Fergus took **drawing the** **them with** **and strength that** **he knew what she was going through. That he understood.**

Which was an illusion. No one knew what she was going through. She didn't understand it herself. She felt herself being drawn. She had no strength to fight him. She'd been fighting to be solitary for so long—to stay aloof.

She didn't need this man to hug her. She didn't need anyone. But she didn't fight him. For this moment she needed him too much. Human contact. That was all it was, she thought fiercely. Warmth and strength and reassurance. It was an illusion, she knew, but for now...

For now she let herself be held. She let her body melt against his, letting him take a weight that had suddenly seemed unbearable. He was strong and firm and warm. His lips were touching her hair.

She should pull away, but she couldn't. For now she needed this too much.

Marion Lennox is a country girl, born on a south-east Australian dairy farm. She moved on—mostly because the cows just weren't interested in her stories! Married to a 'very special doctor', Marion writes for Medical Romance™ as well as Tender Romance™, where she used to write as Trisha David for a while. In her non-writing life, Marion cares for kids, cats, dogs, chooks and goldfish. She travels, and she fights her rampant garden (she's losing) and her house dust (she's lost). After an early bout with breast cancer she's also reprioritised her life, figured out what's important, and discovered the joys of deep baths, romance and chocolate. Preferably all at the same time!

Recent titles by the same author:

THE DOCTOR'S PROPOSAL
HIS SECRET LOVE-CHILD*
BRIDE BY ACCIDENT
THE DOCTOR'S SPECIAL TOUCH

Crocodile Creek 24-hour Rescue

RESCUE AT CRADLE LAKE

BY
MARION LENNOX

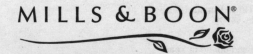

First published in Great Britain 2006
Harlequin Mills & Boon Limited,
Eton House, 18-24 Paradise Road, Richmond, Surrey TW9 1SR

© Marion Lennox 2006

ISBN-13: 978 0 263 84758 1
ISBN-10:   0 263 84758 6

Set in Times Roman 10½ on 11 pt
03-1006-54599

Printed and bound in Spain
by Litografia Rosés, S.A., Barcelona

RESCUE AT
CRADLE LAKE

PROLOGUE

HE MADE the decision at two in the morning. There'd been no serious car crashes in the last few hours. No appendices or aneurisms, no ruptures, assaults or dramas. Night shift at City Central was deathly quiet.

He wanted it to be more so. No less than four nurses and one intern had used the lull to ask him how he was coping. 'No, really, Dr Reynard, if you'd like to talk about it…'

He didn't. He glowered at everyone who came close, he settled himself in the staff lounge, and he concentrated on his reading. Specifically, he concentrated on reading the 'Appointments Vacant' in this month's medical journal.

'Where's Dimboola?'

'My aunty lives in Dimboola,' one of the theatre nurses ventured. 'It's in North West Victoria. Aunty Liz says it's a great little town.'

'Right,' he said, and struck a line through Dimboola. There was silence while he checked a few more ads. Then: 'Where's Mission Beach?'

'North Queensland,' the same nurse told him. 'You remember Joe and Jodie?'

'Joe and Jodie?'

'Joe was the paediatric intern here last year. Big, blond guy almost as hunky as you. Six feet tall and yummy—every sensible woman's dream.' She grinned, but in a way that said her compliment wasn't idle banter but was designed to cheer him up. As was everything anyone said to him at the moment. *Let's look after Fergus...*

'Joe married Jodie Walters from ICU,' she continued, as she failed to elicit a smile. 'They took a job at Port Douglas last year and that's close to Mission Beach.'

OK. Fergus sorted the dross and came up with the information he needed. There were people he knew close to Mission Beach.

Another line.

He knew the next place in the list of advertisements, and the next, and the next. More advertisements were consigned to oblivion. Then: 'Where's Cradle Lake?'

Silence.

This was hopeful. He gazed around, checking each of his colleagues for any sign of recognition. 'Does anyone know where Cradle Lake is?'

'Never heard of it,' Graham, his anaesthetist, told him. 'Cradle Mountain's in Tasmania. Is it near there?'

'Apparently not. It has a New South Wales postcode'

'Never heard of it, then.'

'No one knows it?' Fergus demanded, and received four shakes of four heads in reply.

'Great,' he said, and the line became a circle. 'That's where I'm going.'

Ginny got the phone call at two in the morning. She'd known it had been coming, but it didn't make it any less appalling.

Richard was ringing from his hospital bed. He hadn't wanted her with him when he was told, and he'd waited until now to call.

Who could blame him? Where could anyone find the courage to face news like this, much less pass it on?

'They can't do another transplant,' he said, in a voice devoid of all emotion. 'The specialists say there's no hope it'll work.'

'I guessed it must be that,' she whispered. 'When you didn't call earlier, I thought it must be bad news. Oh, Richard.' She sat up in bed, trying not to cry. 'I'll come.'

'No. Not now.'

'What are you doing?'

'Staring at the ceiling. Wondering how I'm going to face what's coming. And whether I have the right to ask…'

'To ask what?'

'Ginny, I want to go home. Back to Cradle Lake.'

She drew in her breath at that. She hadn't been near Cradle Lake for years.

Richard had referred to Cradle Lake as home. Home was where the heart was, she thought dumbly. Home surely wasn't at Cradle Lake.

'Richard, there are no medical facilities at Cradle Lake. I don't think there's even a doctor there any more.'

'The time for the clever stuff is over,' he said, so roughly that he made himself gasp for breath. It took him a moment or two to recover, gaining strength for the next thought. 'I just need… I just need to know it'll be OK. Surely having a doctor for a sister has to count for something. You can do what's necessary.'

'I don't know that I can.'

'You can keep me pain-free?'

There was only one answer to that. The medical part was the least of what she was facing, and it wasn't her medical skills she was doubting. 'Yes.'

'Well, then.'

'Richard, the house…' Her mind was spinning at tangents, trying to find a way out of what was inescapable. 'It's been neglected for years.'

'You can get it fit for us. If I stay in hospital for a few more days, you'll have time to organise it. We don't need luxury. I'm prepared to stay here until the weekend.'

Gee, thanks, she thought, her mind churning through grief, through shock and confusion, surfacing suddenly with anger. He'd wait while she quit the job she loved. While she packed up her apartment. While she salvaged the wreck of a house she hated, and while she moved her life back to a place she loathed.

But at least she had a life. She closed her eyes, willing anger to retreat. She knew from experience that anger made pain recede. That was why she was feeling it now, but in the long term anger didn't help anything. Pain would always surface.

She couldn't let her anger show. Nor her pain.

'Are you sure you want to do this?' she managed, and was thankful she was on the end of the phone and not by her brother's bedside. She didn't want him to see her like this. She was trembling all over, shaking as if she'd been placed on ice.

'I'm sure,' he said, more strongly. 'I'm going to sit on our back veranda and...'

His voice broke off. He didn't have to finish. They both knew the word that would finish the sentence. This was a family song, sung over and over.

'Will you do this for me, Ginny?' he asked in a voice that had changed, and once again there was only one reply.

'Of course I will,' she managed. 'You know I will.'

She always had, she thought, but she didn't say it. There was no point in saying what they both knew.

The cost of life was losing.

CHAPTER ONE

SHE was lying where he wanted to drive.

Dr Fergus Reynard was lost. He'd been given a map of sealed roads, but sealed roads accounted for about one per cent of the tracks around here. Take the second track left over the ridge, the district nurse had told him, and he'd stared at wheel marks and tried to decide which was a track and which was just the place where some obscure vehicle had taken a jaunt through the mud after the last rain.

Somewhere around here, someone called Oscar Bentley, was lying on his kitchen floor with a suspected broken hip. Oscar needed a doctor. Him. The hospital Land Cruiser had lost traction on the last turn. He'd spun and when he'd corrected there had been a woman lying across the road.

The woman wasn't moving. She was face down over some sort of cattle grid. He could see tight jeans—so tight he knew it was definitely a woman. He could see ancient boots. She was wearing an even more ancient windcheater, and her caramel-blonde, shoulder-length curls were sprawled out around her.

Why was she lying on the road? He was out of the truck, reaching her in half a dozen strides, expecting the worst. Had she collapsed? Had she been hit before he'd arrived? He knelt, his medical training switching into overdrive.

'At last,' she muttered, as he touched her shoulder. 'Whoever you are, can you grab its other ear?'

Medical training took a step back. 'Um… Pardon?'

'Its ear,' she said. Her voice was muffled but she still managed to sound exasperated. 'My arm's not long enough to get a decent hold. I can reach one ear but not the other. I've been lying here for half an hour waiting for the football to finish, and if you think I'm letting go now you've another think coming.'

He needed to take in the whole situation. Woman lying face down over a cattle grid. Arm down through the grid.

He stared down through the bars.

She was holding what looked like a newborn lamb by the tip of one ear. The ear was almost two feet down, underneath the row of steel rails.

The pit was designed to stop livestock passing from one property to another. A full-grown sheep couldn't cross this grid. A newborn lamb couldn't cross the grid either, but this one had obviously tried. It was so small it had simply slipped through to the pit below.

OK. Trapped lamb. Girl lying on road. Fergus's training was asserting itself. In an emergency he'd been taught to take in the whole situation before doing anything.

Make sure there's no surrounding danger before moving into help mode.

On top of the ridge stood a ewe, bleating helplessly. She was staring down at them as if they were enemies—as if she'd like to ram them.

Did sheep ram anyone?

The girl obviously wasn't worried about ramming sheep, so maybe he shouldn't either. But maybe continuing to lie in the middle of the road wasn't such a great idea.

'I could have hit you,' he said. Then, as she didn't answer, anxiety gave way to anger. 'I could have run you over. Are you out of your mind?'

'No one drives fast on this track unless they're lunatics,' she muttered, still clutching the lamb's ear. 'Sane drivers always slow down at cattle grids.'

That pretty much put him in his place.

'Do you intend to stand there whinging about where I

should or shouldn't lie, or are you going to help me?' the woman demanded, and he decided maybe he should do something.

'What do you want me to do?'

'Squeeze your arm through the bars and catch the other ear.'

'Right.' Maybe that was easier said than done. The woman was finely built, which was why she'd been able to reach the lamb. It'd be a harder call for someone heavier. Someone with a thicker arm. Like him. 'Then what?' he said cautiously.

'I can't get my other arm into position. If I release this ear, he'll bolt to the other side of the pit and it'll take me ages to catch him again. If you can grab his other ear and pull him up for a moment, I reckon I can reach further down and get him by the scruff of the neck.'

'And pull him out?'

She sighed. 'That's the idea, Einstein.'

'There's no need—'

'To be rude. No,' she agreed. 'Neither is there any need for me to rescue this stupid lamb. It's not even my lamb. But I just walked out to catch some bucolic air and I heard him bleating. It's taken ages to catch him and he'll die if I leave him. I've been in the one spot for half an hour waiting for the footy to finish so someone would come along this damned road—and the iron's digging into my face—so can we cut it out with the niceties and grab the stupid ear?'

'Right,' he said, and rolled up his sleeves.

It was even harder than he'd thought. He had muscles, built from years of gym work at his well-equipped city hospital, and those muscles didn't help now. Up to his elbow was easy but then he had to shove hard and it hurt, and even then he could only just touch.

'Jump!' the woman yelled, and he and the lamb both jumped—which gave him access to an extra inch of ear. He got a hold.

They were now lying sprawled over the cattle grid with a lamb's ear each. Neat, Fergus thought, and turned to grin at her.

She wasn't grinning. She was pressed hard against him,

her body warm against his, and she was concentrating solely on sheep.

'Let go and you're dead meat,' she muttered. 'On the count of three, we pull our ears up.'

'We'll break its neck.'

'I only want to pull him up a couple of inches or so, in a nice smooth pull—no jerking—and then I'll grab his neck. If I try and pull by one ear, I'll break his neck. Ready, set... Now!'

What happened to the one, two, three? But he was ready and he'd gone beyond arguing. He tugged the lamb upward, she grabbed—and somehow she had a handful of wool at the back of the little creature's neck.

Then she had more orders.

'Shove your hand under its belly,' she gasped, as she tugged the creature higher, and he did and thirty seconds later they had a shivery, skinny, still damply newborn lamb rising out of the pit into the late afternoon sun.

'Oh, hooray,' the woman whispered. She struggled to her feet, cradling the lamb against her, and for the first time Fergus managed to get a proper look at her.

She was in her late twenties, he thought, deciding she wasn't a whole lot younger than his thirty-four years. She was five feet four or five, dressed in ancient jeans and an even more ancient windcheater. Her tousled curls were blowing everywhere. Freckles were smattered over a pert and pretty nose. She was liberally mud-spattered, but somehow the mud didn't matter. She was patting the lamb, but her clear brown eyes were assessing him with a candour that made him feel disconcerted.

She was *some* package.

'You're not a local,' she said, and he realised she'd been doing the same assessment as him.

'I'm the local doctor.'

She'd been trying to stop the lamb from struggling as she ran her hands expertly over its body. She was doing an assessment for damage, he thought, but now her hand stopped in mid-stroke.

'The local doctor's dead.'

'Old Doc Beaverstock died five years ago,' he agreed. 'The people who run the hospital seem to think they need a replacement. That's me. Speaking of which, can you tell me—?'

'You're working here?'

'As of yesterday, yes.'

Her eyes closed and when they opened again he saw a wash of pain. And something more. Relief?

'Oh, thank God,' she said. Then she set the lamb onto its feet and let it go.

The place where they were standing was deserted. To the west lay lush paddocks any self-respecting sheep would think were sheep paradise. To the west was the ewe. To the east was the cattle pit and dense bushland leading down to a lake formed by an ancient volcano.

West or east?

Some actions were no-brainers. The lamb turned and ducked through the woman's legs, straight for the cattle pit.

'Stop,' she screamed, and not for nothing had Fergus played rugby for his university. He took a flying tackle and caught the creature by a back hoof as it hit the first rail.

Face down in the mud he lay, holding onto the leg for dear life.

'Oh, well done.' She was laughing, kneeling in the mud beside him, gathering the lamb back into her arms again, and he thought suddenly, She smells nice. Which was ridiculous. In truth, she smelt of lamb and mud with the odd spot of manure thrown in. How could she smell nice?

'Don't let him go again,' he said weakly, wiping mud from his face as he shoved himself into a sitting position. He'd hit the ground hard and he was struggling to get his breath.

'I'm so sorry.' She rose and grinned down at him, and she didn't look sorry at all.

She had a great grin.

'Think nothing of it,' he managed. 'Take the damned thing away.'

'I haven't got a car.' Holding the lamb in one arm, she offered a hand to help haul him to his feet. He took it and discovered she was surprisingly strong. She tugged, and he rose, and suddenly she was just…close. Nice, he thought inconsequentially. Really nice. 'I'm about half a mile from where I live,' she was saying, but suddenly he was having trouble hearing.

'So?' He was disconcerted. The feel of her hand… Yep, he was definitely disconcerted. She released him and he was aware of a pang of loss.

She didn't seem to notice. She was looking up toward the ewe, brushing mud from her face and leaving more mud in its place. 'It was dumb to let him go,' she muttered. 'He and his mum need to go in the house paddock until we're sure he's recovered.'

'How do you get them to a house paddock?' Fergus asked, and then thought maybe that was a question he shouldn't have asked. It was tantamount to offering help.

And here it came. The request.

She bit her lip. 'I don't think I can herd a sheep and a lamb up to the house,' she admitted. 'Ewes aren't like cows. They might or might not follow, even if I have the lamb.' She looked at his Land Cruiser and he saw exactly what she was thinking. 'Can you give me a lift to the Bentley place? That's where these two belong.'

'Oscar Bentley's?' he demanded, startled.

'Yes.' She handed him the lamb and he was so astounded that he took it. 'Just stand there and don't move,' she told him. Then: 'No,' she corrected herself. 'Joggle up and down a bit, so the ewe's looking at you and not me.'

'I need to go.' He was remembering Oscar Bentley. Yes, the lamb's needs were urgent, but a broken hip was more so.

'Not until we have the ewe.' She moved swiftly away, twenty, thirty yards up the slope, moving with an ease that was almost catlike. Then she disappeared behind a tree and he realised what she was doing.

He was being used as a distraction.

OK, he could do that. Obediently he held the lamb toward

the ewe. The ewe stared wildly down at her lamb and took a tentative step forward.

The woman launched herself out from behind her tree in a rugby tackle that put Fergus's efforts to shame. The ewe was big, but suddenly she was propped up on her rear legs, which prevented her from struggling, and the woman had her solidly and strongly in position.

It had been a really impressive manoeuvre. To say Fergus was impressed was an understatement.

'Put the lamb in your truck and back it up to me,' she told him, gasping with effort, and he blinked.

'Um…'

'I can't stand here for ever.' If she'd had a foot free, she would have stamped it. 'Move.'

He moved.

He was about to put a sheep in the back of the hospital truck.

Fine. As of two days ago he was a country doctor. This was the sort of thing country doctors did. Wasn't it?

It seemed it was. This country doctor had no choice.

He hauled open the back of the truck, shoved the medical equipment as far forward as it'd go and tossed a canvas over the lot. Miriam, his practice nurse, had set the truck up for emergencies and she had three canvases folded and ready at the side. For coping with sheep?

Maybe Miriam knew more about country practice than he did.

Anyone would know more about country practice than he did.

He put the lamb in the back and started closing the door, but as he did so the little creature wobbled. He hesitated.

He sighed and lifted the lamb out again. He climbed in behind the wheel and placed the lamb on his knee.

'Don't even think about doing anything wet,' he told it. 'House-training starts now.'

The woman was walking the sheep down the slope toward the track. He backed up as close as he could.

'Mess my seat and you're chops,' he told the lamb in a further refinement of house-training. He closed the door firmly on one captive and went to collect another.

Getting the ewe into the truck was no easy task. The ewe took solid exception to being manhandled, but the woman seemed to have done this many times before. She pushed, they both heaved, and the creature was in. The door slammed, and Fergus headed for the driver's door in relief.

The woman was already clambering into the passenger seat, lifting the lamb over onto her knee. Wherever they were going, it seemed she was going, too.

'I can drop them at Bentley's,' he told her. 'That's where I'm going.'

'You're going to Bentley's?'

'That's the plan.' He hesitated. 'But I'm a bit lost.'

'Go back the way you came,' she said, snapping her seat belt closed under the lamb. 'I can walk home from there. It's close. Take the second turn to the left after the ridge.'

'That's the second time I've been given that direction,' he told her. 'Only I'm facing the opposite way.'

'You came from the O'Donell track to get to Oscar's?'

'I'm not a local,' he said, exasperated.

'You're the local doctor.'

I'm here as a locum. I've been here since Thursday and I'll be here for twelve weeks.'

She stared and he thought he could see calculations happening behind her eyes.

'That might be long enough,' she whispered, and he thought she was talking to the lamb. She was hugging it close—two muddy waifs.

He wasn't exactly pristine himself.

Whatever she was thinking, though, she didn't expand on it. They drove for a couple of minutes in silence and he realised he didn't even know her name

I'm Dr Fergus Reynard,' he told her, into what had suddenly become a tense stillness.

'I'm Ginny Viental.'

'Ginny?'

'Short for Guinevere, but I'm not exactly Guinevere material.'

Hadn't Guinevere been some gorgeous queen? If that was the case...

But maybe she was right, Fergus decided. Maybe Queen Guinevere wouldn't be splodged with lamb mud.

But there was definitely gorgeous underneath the mud.

'I'm pleased to meet you, Ginny,' he told her, figuring he should concentrate on keeping the truck on the slippery track rather than letting his attention stray to this very different woman beside him. It was a hard task. 'Do you live around here?'

'I used to live here,' she told him. 'I've just come back... for a while.'

'Do your parents live here?'

'They lived here when I was a kid,' she said discouragingly. 'I did, too, until I was seventeen.'

She wasn't seventeen now, he thought, trying again to figure her age. She looked young but there were lines around her eyes that made him think she'd not had things easy. But something in her face precluded him from asking questions.

'Oscar Bentley,' he said cautiously, searching for neutral ground. 'You're sure it's his lamb?'

'I'm sure. The cattle grid's on our property but he has agistment rights. Oscar was an ordinary farmer fifteen years back. Now he seems to have lost the plot completely.'

'He's hardly made a decent access track,' Fergus muttered, hauling the truck away from an erosion rut a foot deep.

'He likes making it hard for visitors,' Ginny told him. 'Why has he called you out? Unless that's breaking patient confidentiality.'

'I'm not sure there can be much patient confidentiality about a broken hip.'

'A broken hip?'

'That's what he thinks is wrong.'

She snorted. 'Yeah, right. Broken hip? I'll bet he's fallen down drunk and he wants someone to put him to bed.'

'You know him well, then?'

'I told you, I lived here. I haven't been near Oscar for years but he won't have changed.'

'If you don't live here now, where do you live?'

'Will you quit it with the inquisition?' she said, her voice muffled by the lamb again. 'I hate the smell of wet wool.'

'So don't stick your nose into wet sheep.'

'There's a medical prescription for you,' she said and she grinned. Which somehow…changed things again.

Wow, he thought. That was *some* smile. When the lines of strain eased from around her eyes she looked…beautiful?

Definitely beautiful.

'Why are you here?' she demanded, hauling her nose off the lamb as if the question had only just occurred to her and it was important.

'I told you. I'm here as a locum.'

'We've never been able to get a locum before.'

'I can't imagine why not,' he said with asperity, releasing the brakes then braking again to try and get some traction on the awful track. 'This is real resort country. Not!'

'You're seeing it at its worst. We had a doozy of a storm last week and the flooding's only just gone down.'

'It's not bad,' he conceded, staring out at the rolling hills and bushland and the deep, clear waters of the lake below. Sure, it was five hours' drive to the nearest city, to the nearest specialist back-up, but that was what he'd come for. Isolation. And the rugged volcanic country had a beauty all its own. 'Lots of…sheep,' he said cautiously.

'Lots of sheep,' she agreed, looking doubtfully out the window as if she was trying to see the good side, too.

'If you think sheep are pretty.'

She twisted to look over her shoulder at the morose-looking ewe in the back of the truck. As if on cue, the creature widened her back legs and let go a stream of urine.

'Oh, yeah,' she agreed. 'Sheep. My favourite animals.'

He was going to have to clean out the back of his truck. Already the pungent ammoniac smell was all around them. Despite that, his lips twitched.

'A farmer, born and bred.'

'I'm no farmer,' she said.

'Which might explain why you were lying on the road in the middle of nowhere, holding a lamb by one ear, when the entire crowd from the Cradle Lake football game could have come by at any minute and squashed you.'

There was that grin again. 'The entire crowd from this side of the lake being exactly eight locals, led by Doreen Kettle who takes her elderly mother and her five kids to the football every week and who drives ten times slower than you. The last of the eight will be the coach who drives home about ten tonight. Cradle Lake will have lost—we always lose—and our coach will have drowned his sorrows in the pub. There'll be no way he'll be on the roads until after the Cradle Lake constabulary go to bed. Which is after *Football Replay* on telly, which finishes at nine-thirty, leaving the rest of Saturday night for Cradle Lake to make whoopee.'

'How long did you say you've been away?' he asked cautiously, and she chuckled. It was a very nice chuckle, he decided. Light and soft and gurgling. Really infectious.

'Ten years. But nothing, nothing, nothing changes in Cradle Lake. Even Doreen Kettle's kids. When I left she was squashing them into the back of the car to take them to the footy. They're still squashing, only the squashing's got tricker. I think the youngest is now six feet three.' She brightened. 'But, then, you've changed. Cradle Lake has a doctor. Why are you here?'

He sighed. The question was getting repetitive. 'I told you—as a locum.'

'No one's ever been able to get a locum for Cradle Lake before. The last doctor was only here because his car broke down here just after the war. He was on his way to visit a war buddy and he couldn't get anyone to repair it. He didn't have the gumption to figure any other way of moving on.'

Fergus winced. He'd only been in the district for a couple of days but already the stories of the old doctor's incompetence were legion.

'Your truck's still operating,' Ginny pointed out. 'So why did you stop?'

'This is the hospital truck. And I ran my finger down the ads in the medical journal and chose the first place I'd never heard of.'

She stared. 'Why?'

'I wanted a break from the city.'

She eyed him with caution. 'You realise you won't exactly get a holiday here. This farming land's marginal. You have a feeder district of very poor families who'll see your presence as a godsend. You'll be run off your feet with medical needs that have needed attention for years.'

'I want to be busy.'

She considered him some more and he wondered what she was seeing. His reasons for coming? He hoped not. He tried to keep his face expressionless.

'So, by break,' she said cautiously, 'you don't mean a break from medicine.'

'No.'

She eyed him for a bit longer, but somewhat to his surprise she didn't ask any more questions. Maybe she didn't want him asking questions back, he thought, and he glanced at her again and knew he was right. There was something about the set of her face that said her laughter was only surface deep. There were problems. Real and dreadful problems.

As a good physician he should probe.

No. He wasn't a good physician. He was a surgeon and he was here as a locum, to focus on superficial problems and refer anything worse to the city.

He needed to think about a fractured hip.

They were bumping over yet another cattle grid. Before them was a ramshackle farmhouse, surrounded by what looked like a graveyard for ancient cars. About six ill-assorted, half-starved dogs were on the veranda, and they came tearing down the ramp baying like the hounds from hell as the vehicle pulled to a stop.

'I'm a city boy,' Fergus said nervously, staring out at the

snarling mutts, and Ginny grinned, pushed open the door and placed the lamb carefully on her seat behind her. She closed the truck door as the hounds reached her, seemingly ready to tear her to pieces.

'Sit,' she roared, in a voice that could have been heard in the next state. They all backed off as if she'd tossed a bucket of cold water over them. Three of the mongrels even sat, and a couple of them wagged their disreputable tails.

She swiped her hands together in a gesture of a job well done and then turned and peeped a smile at him.

'You can get out now,' she told him. 'The dragons have been slain. And we're quits. You rescued me and I've rescued you right back.'

'Thanks,' he told her, stepping gingerly out—but all the viciousness of the dogs had been blasted out of them.

But the dogs were the least of his problems. 'Doc?' It was a man's voice, coming from the house, and it was a far cry from the plaintive tone that had brought him here in the first place. 'Is that the bloody doctor?' the voice yelled. 'About bloody time. A man could die…' The voice broke off in a paroxysm of coughing, as if the yell had been a pent-up surge of fury that had left the caller exhausted.

'Let's see the patient,' Ginny said, heading up the ramp before him.

Who was the doctor here? Feeling more at sea than he'd ever felt in his entire medical training, Fergus was left to follow.

Oscar Bentley was a seriously big man. Huge. He'd inched from overweight to obese many years ago, Fergus thought as a fast visual assessment had him realising the man was in serious trouble.

Maybe that trouble didn't stem from a broken hip, but he was in trouble nevertheless. He lay like a beached whale, sprawled across the kitchen floor. A half-empty carton of beer lay within reach so he hadn't been in danger of dying from thirst, but he certainly couldn't get up. His breathing was rasping, each breath sucked in as if it took a conscious effort to haul in enough air. The indignant roar he'd made as they'd arrived must have been a huge effort.

Ginny reached his patient before him. 'Hey, Oscar, Doc Reynard tells me you've broken your hip.' She was bending over the huge man, lifting his wrist. 'What a mess.'

The elderly man's eyes narrowed. He looked like he'd still like to yell but the effort seemed beyond him. His breathing was dangerously laboured, yet anger seemed tantamount.

'You're one of the Viental kids,' he snarled. 'What are you doing here?'

'I'm Ginny,' she agreed cordially, and to Fergus's astonishment she was looking at her watch as her fingers rested on the man's wrist. Did she have medical training?

'A Viental,' the farmer gasped, and he groaned as he shifted his vast bulk to look at her more closely. 'What the hell are you doing on my property? Why aren't you dead?'

'I'm helping Doc Reynard. Plus I pulled one of your lambs out of the cattle grid dividing your land from ours.' Her face hardened a little. 'I've been up on the ridge, looking over the stock you've been running on our land. Your ewes have obviously been lambing for weeks and at least six ewes have died during lambing. They've been left where they died. No one's been near them.'

'Mind your own business,' he gasped. 'I didn't call Doc Reynard for a lecture—and I didn't call you. I don't want a Viental anywhere near my property.'

'You called Doc Reynard to get you on your feet again,' she snapped. 'There's no way he can do that on his own—without a crane, that is.'

'Let's check the hip,' Fergus said uneasily, and she flashed a look of anger back at him.

'There's no difference in the length of Oscar's legs. He has breathing difficulties but that's because he won't do anything about his asthma. He'll have got himself into this state because he couldn't be bothered fending for himself so he feels like a few days in the hospital. He does it deliberately and he's been doing it for twenty years.' She glanced around the kitchen and winced. 'Though by the look of it, it's gone beyond the need for a few days in hospital now. Maybe we need to talk about a nursing home.'

She had a point. The place was disgusting. But still…

'The hip,' Fergus reiterated, trying again to regain control.

'Right. The hip.' She sat back and pressed her fingers lightly on Oscar's hips. 'How about that?' she said softly, while both men stared at her, astounded. 'No pain?'

'Aagh!' Oscar roared, but the roar was a fraction too late.

Enough. He was the doctor and this was his patient. 'Do you mind moving back?' he demanded, lifting Ginny's hands clear. 'I need to do an examination.'

'There's no need. He'll have stopped taking his asthma medication. Do you want me to get oxygen from your truck?'

'I was called to a broken hip,' Fergus said testily. He didn't have a clue what was happening here—what the dynamics were. Her pressure on the hips without result had been diagnosis enough, but he wasn't taking chances on a patient—and a situation—that he didn't know. 'Let me examine him.'

Almost surprisingly she agreed. 'I'll get the oxygen and then I'll wait outside. I'll take care of the sheep. Someone's got to take care of the sheep. Then I'll come with you to the hospital.'

He frowned. He wasn't too sure why she intended coming to the hospital. He wasn't even sure he wanted her. There was something about this woman's presence that was sending danger signals, thick and fast. 'You were going to walk home.'

'He'll have to go to hospital,' she said evenly. 'He's drunk, his breathing's unstable, and you won't be able to prove he hasn't got a broken hip without X-rays. How are you planning to lift Oscar yourself?'

'I'll call in the paramedics,' he snapped.

'Excuse me, but this is the last home and away football match for Cradle Lake this season,' Ginny snapped back. 'If by paramedic you mean Ern and Bill, who take it in turns to drive the local ambulance, then you'll find they refuse absolutely to come until the match—and the post-match celebration—is over. Especially if it's to come to Oscar.'

Which was why he had come here in the first place, he thought dourly. The call had come in and there'd been no one willing to take it.

'That leaves you stuck,' she continued. 'For a couple of hours at least. Unless you accept help.'

'Fine,' he conceded, trying not to sound confused. 'I'll accept your help. Can you wait outside?'

'Very magnanimous,' she said, and she grinned.

His lips twitched despite his confusion. It was a great grin. Get on with the job. Ignore gorgeous grins.

'Just go,' he told her, and she clicked her disreputable boots together and saluted.

'Yes, sir.'

CHAPTER TWO

SHE went. Fergus did a perfunctory examination and then a more thorough one.

Oscar had no broken hip, but Ginny was right—the man was dead drunk. His blood pressure was up to one ninety on a hundred and ten and his breathing was fast and noisy, even once he was on oxygen. Fergus checked his saturation levels and accepted the inevitable.

'I gotta go to hospital, don't I, Doc?' Oscar demanded, with what was evident satisfaction. His breathing was becoming more shallow now and Fergus wondered whether he'd drunk a lot fast just as they'd arrived—just to make sure. 'I told you I got a broken hip.'

'You don't appear to have broken anything,' Fergus told him. 'But, yes, you need to come to hospital.' He gazed around the kitchen and grimaced. 'Maybe we need to think about some sort of permanent care,' he suggested. 'Unless there's anyone who can stay with you.'

'That's not me,' Ginny said through the screen door. 'Or anyone in this district. This isn't exactly Mr Popular here. What's the prognosis?'

'Mr Bentley needs help with his breathing,' Fergus said, trying not to sound like he was talking through gritted teeth. He knew by now that the diagnosis she'd made had been spot on. 'He's not safe to leave alone. The ambulance will have to come out to collect him.'

'I told you—they won't come for at least a couple of hours.'

'Will you stay with Mr Bentley until they come?' he asked, without much hope, and she shook her head.

'Nope. I'm needed elsewhere and I can't stand Mr Bentley.'

'I can't stand you either, miss,' the farmer snapped. 'You and your whore of a mother. You and your family deserved everything you got.'

Ginny had opened the screen door and stepped inside, but Oscar's words stopped her. She flinched, recoiling as if she had been struck. Her colour faded and she leaned back against the kitchen bench as if she suddenly needed support.

'No family ever deserved what happened to us,' she whispered, and she turned to Fergus as if she couldn't bear the sight of the man on the floor. She swallowed, evidently trying hard to move on from his vicious words. 'Obese patients like him are the pits,' she said, 'and if you leave him alone he'll stay alive just long enough to sue. More's the pity. So you need to take him to hospital. If neither of us want to sit here for a couple of hours, that means we use the back of your truck. I got the ewe out.'

'You got the ewe out,' he said blankly, and she managed a weak smile.

'That would be the sheep, city boy. The one that was…well, making herself at home in the back of your Land Cruiser. I put the ewe and her baby in the home paddock.' She glared down at Oscar with disdain. 'I put hay in there, too, and I filled the trough,' she said. 'Much to the relief of the rest of the stock. You're so off our property. I'd rather let the place go to ruin than let you agist on our place again. The dogs are starving. The sheep are fly-blown and miserable, and there's a horse locked up…' She broke off and Fergus saw real distress on her face. 'I'll get the RSPCA out here straight away,' she whispered, 'and I hope you end up in jail. You deserve to be there. Not hospital.'

Whew. 'Ginny, can we keep to the matter at hand?' Fergus said, trying to keep control in a situation that was spiralling. 'We can't take Mr Bentley in the truck.'

'Sure we can,' Ginny said, making an obvious effort to

shove distress aside. 'I've washed it out—sort of. A nice amniotic smell never hurt anyone. Maybe we could be super-nice and find a mattress. The back of the Land Cruiser is long enough to make an ambulance.'

'But lifting—'

'A stretcher won't do it,' she agreed. 'We'd break both our backs. Hang on for a bit and I'll find a door and some fence posts. And a mattress. Be right back.'

And she was gone, slipping through to the living room and the bedrooms beyond.

'You gonna let her just walk though my house?' Oscar roared—or tried to roar, but the drink and the asthma were taking their toll and he was losing his bluster. His roar was cut off in mid-tirade and the last words were said as a gasp.

'I'm not sure what else to do,' Fergus admitted. 'She's in control and we're not. So you concentrate on your breathing and we'll let Ginny sort us both out.'

His opinions were consolidated five minutes later while he watched, as Ginny attacked the kitchen door. She'd found a mattress and had it lying on the floor beside Oscar. She'd also found three cylindrical fence posts, each about three feet long, and now she was unscrewing door hinges.

'Do you mind letting me in on the plan?' Fergus asked, but Oscar chose that moment to retch and he had to focus on keeping the airway clear.

'He took this too far,' Ginny said briefly, glancing across at their patient with active dislike. 'If you hadn't been available he'd have risked dying. He's played this too many times for the locals to take any notice.'

Fergus sighed. Doctors were trained to save lives, no matter how obnoxious those lives were, but it didn't always feel good. Now he thought longingly about his beautifully equipped city hospital and his wonderfully trained nursing staff who'd cope with the messy bits that he was forced to cope with himself now. Back in Sydney, if a patient retched he'd step back and hand over to the nurses.

'I'm good at woodwork,' he told Ginny without much hope, and she smiled.

'Not in a million years, mate,' she told him. 'I'm on door duty. You're on patient duty.'

Finally the last screw holding the door to the hinge was released. The door fell forward and Ginny grunted in satisfaction as she took its weight.

'Great. I was afraid it'd be solid. This is light enough to give us a bit more leverage.'

'So now what?'

'Let's get it under him,' she told him. 'Is his airway clear?'

'As good as I can get.' Oscar was drifting into alcoholic sleep, which at least meant that they could work without abuse.

'We'll leave the oxygen on till the last moment,' Ginny told him. 'He'll have to be unhooked for a bit while we load him into the truck. But we'll work fast.'

'Are you medical?' he asked, bemused, but she wasn't listening. She was sliding the door toward him, signalling him to shove the other end as close as he could to Oscar.

Then she hauled the mattress on top.

'Put this pillow between his hips in case he really has got a broken bone,' she ordered, and he stopped wondering whether she had a medical background. He was sure.

'Now.' Fergus was on one side of Oscar. Ginny was on the other with the door-cum-stretcher between Ginny and Oscar. 'Roll him sideways as far as you can toward you,' she said. 'One hand on his shoulder, the other just above his hip. Don't try and lift—you're just rolling. And I'll shove.'

'Where did you learn to do this?'

'I had a different childhood,' she said. 'I played doctors a lot, and moving patients was my specialty. Shut up and roll.'

So he rolled and she shoved and a moment later their patient was three-quarters on the door.

'Great,' she muttered, completely intent on the job at hand. 'Now we slide. You do the shoulders, I'll do the pelvis. Let's keep those hips in a straight line.'

'Yes, ma'am,' he uttered under his breath, but he didn't say

it. Where did her knowledge come from? Even with knowledge, Oscar was huge. How could she do it?

She did it. Fergus was getting more and more gobsmacked
by the minute. Her strength was amazing.

They now had their patient fully on the door.

'Now we tie him on,' she said, producing something that
looked like frayed hay bands. 'I'm not going to all this trouble
to let him roll off.'

So they tied, sliding the ropes under the door and fasten-
ing them across his legs, hips and stomach. Oscar grunted a
few times but he seemed to be intent now on his breathing—
which was just as well. They completed six ties before Ginny
declared them ready.

'You're not proposing to lift this,' Fergus muttered,
knowing that lifting only one end was beyond him.

'Trust a man to think of brawn when there's brains at
hand,' she told him. She disappeared briefly outside and
came back carrying something that looked dangerously
like an axe.

'Hey! I'm not sure about operating here and axes aren't my
tool of choice,' Fergus told her, startled, and she grinned.

'This is a splitter for chopping wood. Or it's a really neat
wedge.' She laid it sideways so the edge of the splitter lay
under a corner of the door. She put her weight behind the
handle and tugged it in a quarter-circle.

The splitter dug under the door and the corner rose.

'I'll keep shoving and you stick in a pole,' she ordered and
he was with her. The fence posts….long cylinders, ready to
roll, were lined up, ready to insert under the door.

'I'll operate the axe, though,' he told her, seeing her strain
to get the sedge further in. Enough was enough. He had to be
stronger than she was.

He had to be something more than she was.

Whoever, whatever, the plan worked. Two minutes later
they had three poles under the door. At first push the door
started rolling, with Fergus and Ginny carefully manoeuvring
it toward the back door.

'What's happening?' Oscar muttered, sluggish and barely conscious.

Fergus was hauling a pole out at the back of the door, to carry it forward so it became the front roller. 'You're going for a ride,' he told him. 'Courtesy of the most amazing ambulance officer I've ever met. And the most amazing trolley.'

It worked.

Luckily Oscar had a ramp instead of steps leading to the veranda and the only hard part was keeping the thing from sliding too fast. The dogs watched from a distance, seemingly almost as bemused as Fergus.

Then there was the little matter of getting their makeshift stretcher into the truck, but they did that working as a team, finding wedges and chocks of different sizes in the woodshed, tying the ropes under Oscar's arms tighter so he couldn't slip, gradually levering up the end of the door to a new level, chocking, levering again until finally the door reached the height of the floor of the truck.

That was the only time when they needed real strength. There was a moment when they had to take a side apiece and shove.

'One, two three…'

The door slid in like a dream.

'This place stinks,' Oscar said clearly through his mist of alcohol and confusion, and Fergus climbed up beside him to administer oxygen again and tried not to flinch at the by now awful smell in the rear. Oscar was no pristine patient and the ewe's legacy was disgusting.

But it was Oscar's ewe. Ginny's phrase came back to him. She'd just walked out to take in some bucolic air? 'It's good bucolic air,' he told Oscar, trying not to grin. Ginny was still outside the truck, and she, too, was smiling her satisfaction. It had been a neat piece of engineering and they deserved to be pleased with each other. 'Ms. Viental, wasn't that what you were stepping out to find this afternoon? There's lots of it in here. Would you like to ride in the back with our patient while I drive?'

But Ginny was already swinging herself into the driver's seat, reaching over to the back and holding out her hand for the keys.

'You're the doctor,' she said sweetly. 'I'm just part of the bucolic scenery.'

They made a stop on the way that Fergus hadn't planned on.

I can't go straight to the hospital,' Ginny told him as they left Oscar's farm behind them. 'Richard will be worried.'

'Richard?'

'I told him I'd be gone for an hour and it's been two already.' She was driving more competently than he'd been, steering the truck with a skill that told him she'd spent years coping with eroded country tracks.

Where had she learned ambulance skills? Her farming skills? What else did she have going for her?

Gorgeous figure? Lovely complexion? Good sense of humour?

He had to concentrate on his patient.

Luckily, that wasn't too difficult. Oscar was rolling from side to side, fighting against the straps, and Fergus was starting to get really concerned. If he had a broken hip he'd be in agony, the way he was moving. OK, he didn't have a broken hip, but Fergus was starting to worry that the man's blood alcohol level was dangerously high. He reeked of beer and whisky, and his breathing was getting weaker.

'We need to get to the hospital fast,' he told Ginny. 'Ring Richard from the hospital.'

'No can do,' she told him, and turned off the main track onto an even smaller one.

Where was she going? 'I need ICU facilities,' he told her. 'We can't delay.'

'I know it's not optimal care.' She was intent on the track. 'But Oscar's played ducks and drakes with his health for years. If I hadn't been there today, you wouldn't have him this close to the hospital now. I've sped you up a heap. It'll take me two minutes to check on Richard, and I am going to check.'

'Phone him.'

'Go to hell.'

He sat back on his heels and stared through to the cab. He could see her face in the rear-view mirror. All humour had disappeared and her face was tight with strain.

'Is Richard your child?' he asked, confused, and she shook her head.

'Just concentrate on Oscar,' she said tightly. 'Leave Richard to me.'

But somewhere in the haze of alcohol and lack of oxygen Oscar was still hearing. He'd figured what was happening, and he was starting to be scared.

'You get me to hospital,' he breathed, shoving the oxygen mask away so he could make himself heard.

'I'm checking Richard first,' Ginny flung over her shoulder. 'He's just as important as you are.'

'He should be dead. He damn near all but is.'

There was no response. Ginny's hands gripped the steering-wheel so hard her knuckles showed white. She kept on driving but Fergus could see what looked like tears...

'Ginny...'

'Shut up,' she snarled. 'Just shut up and look after Oscar because I'm sure as hell not going to.'

She checked on Richard. Whoever Richard was. Fergus wasn't allowed to know. They pulled to a halt outside a farmhouse that was even more ramshackle than Oscar's. Ginny ran inside, yelling at him not to follow, and, as promised, two minutes later she was back in the cab and the truck was heading back out to the main road.

'Not dead, then?' Oscar wheezed, and the look Fergus caught in the rear-view mirror was one of pure murder.

But now wasn't the time to ask questions, not with Oscar ready to put in his oar and with Ginny's anger threatening to explode. All he could do was keep a lid on it, keep Oscar alive and leave questions for later.

Would he ask the questions?

He wasn't here to get involved, he reminded himself.

What was he here for?

To turn off. To find a place where he could immerse himself so totally in his medicine that everything else would be blocked out.

But the pain on Ginny's face…

It found a reflection in what he'd been through. There was something…

Who was Richard? A husband? An invalid husband?

He wasn't here to get involved.

'I hurt,' the man on the stretcher moaned, and Fergus sighed.

'Where do you hurt?'

'I told you—I smashed my hip.'

Yeah, right. 'I can't give you morphine until the alcohol wears off. And I need to do X-rays.'

'Old doc would'a given me a shot by now.'

'Yeah, he would have shut you up whatever the cost,' Ginny flung at him over her shoulder. 'I can see where he's coming from. Dr Reynard, keep me away from that morphine.'

Cradle Lake Hospital was not exactly the nub of state-of-the-art technology that Fergus was used to.

It had been built fifty or sixty years ago, a pretty little cottage hospital that looked more like a country homestead than a medical facility. Most of the rooms were single, looking out onto the wide verandas that had views down to the lake on one side or up to the vast mountain ranges of the New South Wales snowfields on the other.

It was a great spot for a hospital. Unfortunately, it had been five years since Cradle Lake had been able to attract a doctor, and in those years the place had become little more than a nursing home. Old people came here to die. Patients needing doctors on call were transferred to somewhere with more facilities.

Nevertheless, Fergus had been stunned by the level of care displayed by what seemed an extraordinarily talented pool of local nurses. Being the only hospital for a hundred miles, the local nurses were called on for everything from snakebite to road trauma. They dealt with medicine at the coalface, and from what he'd learned in his two days here, by the time emergency cases were passed over to specialist care, the emergency would often be over.

Miriam, the nurse whose job it was to do home visits and who'd welcomed him with open arms, was waiting as they drove into the entrance to Emergency. A middle-aged farmer's widow, she was as competent as she was matter of fact. Now she came out from the hospital entrance looking worried, and as he emerged from the back of the truck she looked even more worried.

'Where have you been? I should have come with you. Oscar should be in a nursing home. He's not fit to be alone, but I was sure he was putting it on. I would have left him until morning, but you insisted…'

He had insisted. Fergus had been in the call room when Oscar had phoned. Miriam had been inclined to be indignant and let him wait, but Fergus had decided to go anyway.

'He didn't really break a hip, did he?' she demanded, and as Fergus pulled the door of the van wider and she saw their improvised stretcher, she gasped. 'You've brought him in. How—?'

'On a door,' Fergus said, grinning. 'And you're right, he's not fit to be alone. We need to look at a long-term nursing-home option—especially if by going home he gets to be in charge of animals again. Meanwhile, Miriam, we need a proper trolley to get him out of the truck. We need one strong enough to slide Oscar and a door onto. We'll not move him again without a hydraulic lift.'

'Who…?' Miriam asked, and, as if in response to the unfinished question, Ginny jumped out of the cab. Miriam's jaw dropped.

'Ginny,' she gasped. 'Ginny Viental.'

'Hi,' Ginny said, smiling. 'It's Mrs Paterson, isn't it? I remember you. Can you look after Dr Reynard now? I'm going home.'

'Wait and I'll drive you,' Fergus said, still trying to sound as if he was in control, but Ginny shook her head and he knew that control was an illusion.

'I still haven't finished my walk, and Richard's OK for a bit longer. I'll enjoy the hike.'

And then she hesitated.

Until now the valley had been blanketed with the hush of a lazy country Saturday afternoon. Everyone was at the football, watching the football on the telly or starting the hike to bring the cows in for evening milking.

But the hush was broken now by a siren. It started low, a soft rise and fall from the far side of the lake, but it was unmistakable.

'The boys are bringing someone in.' Miriam stared out over the valley as if she was trying to see what was happening. 'There was no callout through here and they haven't radioed in. That means they're both busy. It must be an emergency from the football.'

They regrouped, all of them. A medical team facing a medical crisis. Fergus glanced at Ginny and saw her reacting the same way he was.

'Let's get Oscar stabilised,' Fergus snapped. 'Miriam, fetch a trolley. Ginny, go to Oscar's feet. Move.'

Ginny moved. Miriam moved too and no city hospital could have done it faster. They shoved the door onto a stainless-steel trolley and almost in the same motion they were wheeling it inside. They set Oscar beside a bed in a single ward but there was no time to move him into the bed. Not until they knew what the incoming emergency was.

'Get me into bed,' Oscar muttered, but Fergus was intent on setting up an IV line.

'All in good time,' he muttered. 'You're safe where you are. I need a 5 mil syringe…'

He glanced up, expecting Miriam, but it was Ginny, not Miriam, who was handing him what he needed. While he worked, she was setting up a cardiac monitor and checking the oxygen flow. She'd followed him in behind the trolley and she'd started working without questioning him.

'Miriam's calling in reinforcements,' Ginny told him. 'As she's the only nurse on duty, she might need help. The ambulance boys aren't answering the radio, which makes her think things might be dire.'

'Get me into bed,' Oscar muttered again.

'As soon as we can,' Fergus told him. 'You just lie there and sober up.'

'I'll stay with him until we're sure the oxygen rate's optimal,' Ginny offered, and Fergus hesitated. The siren was so close now that the ambulance would be there in seconds.

But was she qualified? As what?

And there was no love lost between Ginny and Oscar.

'You won't murder him?' he asked, and he was only half joking.

'We've both taken the Hippocratic oath,' Ginny murmured. 'More's the pity.'

His eyebrows took a hike. 'You're a doctor?'

'Only for now,' she said, and her tone was a warning. 'Only when I have to be, so don't get any ideas about weekends off. Now go. Leave Oscar to me and I'll do my best to keep him breathing.'

A doctor?

Fergus made his way swiftly back to Emergency, his mind racing.

Suddenly he felt a whole lot better about what he was facing.

He hadn't thought this through. When Molly had died he'd simply taken the coward's way out. He hadn't been able to stay at his big teaching hospital any more. Everywhere he'd looked there had been memories. And people's eyes… Every time they'd come toward him they'd clapped him on the shoulder or taken his hand and pressed it in gentle empathy. That last day had been unbearable. He'd been performing a simple catheter insertion and the nurse assisting had suddenly choked on a sob and left, leaving the patient sure that there was a disaster his medical team wasn't telling him about—and leaving Fergus sure that he had to leave.

Some of his workmates had been better, he acknowledged. They'd been matter-of-fact, trying not to talk about it—moving on. But the way they'd spoken to him had still been different. He couldn't bear them not talking about it as much as he couldn't bear them talking about it and in the end he hadn't known which he'd hated more.

'Have a break,' his father told him. Jack Reynard was senior cardiologist at the hospital. His father had been caring, but from a distance, all the time Molly had been ill—and after she'd died he'd hardly been able to face Fergus. 'Go lie on the beach for a month or two.'

The thought of lying on any beach without Molly was unbearable but so was staying where he was. So he'd come here. It was only now, hearing the siren, thinking about how truly alone he was, that he wondered how qualified he was to take care of a rural community.

But now he had back-up. Ginny. Whatever her story was.

His strides lengthened. He could cope with whatever it was, he decided. As long as he had another doctor behind him.

Was she nuts, telling him she was a doctor?

Now was hardly the time for recriminations, Ginny decided. There was work to be done and it had to be done fast. The siren meant there was trouble coming and now she'd admitted she had medical training she knew she could be called on to help.

Ginny adjusted Oscar's drip, checked his obs and made him as comfortable as she could without trying to move him. It took two people to use the hydraulic lift, and there weren't two people available. There might not be any people if this was a true emergency on its way here, she thought.

She might be needed but she was concerned about leaving Oscar. The huge man was dead drunk and he could roll off the trolley. If she was called away....

'OK, Viental, do something,' she muttered.

She propped him up on pillows so he was half-sitting. There was no moan as she hauled him up—she'd given the broken hip cursory credence and she gave it even less credence now. He was showing little sign of pain. He'd be safer sitting up if he were to vomit, and X-rays of a possible broken hip would have to wait.

Then she stood back and looked at the bed. The bed had rails, ready to be raised at will. Oscar needed those rails to be safe.

'Right, let's get you organised,' she muttered.

The trolley was resting against the bed, but it couldn't reach the wall at the bedhead because of the bedside table. She could do better than that.

In seconds she was under the bed, grabbing the bedside table and hauling it under. She pushed the head of the trolley hard against the wall at the end of the room, then shoved the trolley sideways till it was against the wall. Which left a foot between bed and trolley.

What was happening outside? Don't ask, she told herself. Get Oscar safe first. She flipped the bed rails up and shoved the bed sideways, securing her patient with the wall on one side of him and the railed bed on the other.

Oscar was now as safe as she could make him, apart from his breathing. But even there… What else could she do? His oxygen was up to maximum. His airway was clear.

He needed supervision, but if there was a greater need and Fergus needed her as a doctor…

'What happens if I want to get out?' Oscar mumbled, but he was so close to sleep she could hardly hear him.

'You're welcome to try,' she told him. 'But I suspect you're trapped. Just like I am.'

'Ginny…' It was a call from the corridor, urgent. Miriam's face appeared round the door. 'Fergus needs you,' she snapped, and disappeared.

'I need to go,' she told Oscar. 'Stay breathing. That's an order.'

'I need a doctor.'

'You've had one,' she told him. 'Relax and let yourself go to sleep.'

'Get lost,' he snapped, and added another word for good measure.

She turned away but she couldn't help but grin. That last expletive had been strong and sure, reassuring her more than anything else that the man might very well survive.

She was right back into medical mode now, almost as if she'd never been away. In truth, the adrenalin surge was there, as it always was in these situations. She'd missed it.

Maybe she could work a little with Fergus.

What sort of man was he?

'Dangerous,' she muttered as she pushed open the swing doors to Emergency, though she wasn't sure why she thought it. But that was her overriding sensation. She'd looked up from the cattle grid as she'd tried to hold onto the lamb, and she'd been caught. Fergus was tall, big-boned and a bit…weathered? He had deep brown hair, crinkly, a little bit too long. It needed a comb. Maybe he raked it with his fingers, she thought inconsequentially. That was what it looked like. His lazy grey eyes held laughter and a certain innate gentleness. He wasn't much older than she was.

He seemed nice.

Definitely dangerous, and she didn't have time in her life for dangerous.

She didn't have any inclination to go down that road. Ever.

CHAPTER THREE

THAT was the last chance Ginny had time to think of the personal for hours.

The moment she opened the doors to Emergency she could see why the ambulance boys hadn't had time to radio in. A woman was lying on the trolley and one glance showed Ginny that they were in trouble. She seemed to be unconscious, limp and flaccid, with each breath shallow and rasping. She was in her late twenties or early thirties, Ginny guessed, simply dressed in faded jeans, white T-shirt and pink sandals. Long blonde hair lay limply around a pallid face and even from the door Ginny could tell that here was a woman who was fighting for her life.

Or maybe here was a woman who'd come to the end.

'Mummy…'

Ginny glanced across to the main entrance to see a little girl being carried in. Four years old, maybe? She looked a waif of a child, tear-streaked and desperate. Her blonde hair, shoulder length, was tied back with a red ribbon with blue elephants on it, but the ribbon was grubby and the curls hadn't been brushed for days. She was wearing shorts and a T-shirt and nothing else.

But it was her feet that caught Ginny's attention. She was barefoot, and her soles seemed to be a mass of lacerations. There was blood on her ankles.

Triage.

Fergus was working over the mother, and he had Miriam and an ambulance officer helping him. The guy holding the child seemed helpless.

Ginny moved at once to the child.

'Mummy,' the little one screamed, every fibre of her body straining toward her mother's trolley.

'Dr Fergus is looking after your mummy,' Ginny told her, but the child was past listening. The ambulance officer was looking to Ginny, desperate to hand over responsibility.

'Give her to me.' Ginny sat on the examination couch and gathered the little girl into her arms.

Miriam was hauling the crash cart toward the trolley and Ginny thought, Uh-oh.

Should she swap places with Miriam? She watched for a minute as the child fought her hold. Miriam looked competent and swift. There was already a cardiac monitor set up. The woman's breathing seemed to be pausing. She was suddenly so limp that Ginny thought, Oh no.

But Fergus was shaking his head at Miriam, signifying the paddles weren't needed. There must be a heartbeat but the expression on Fergus's face as he looked at the monitor…

Ginny knew what that look meant. She'd worked for three years in ER in a major teaching hospital and she knew it all too well.

Triage. The child's feet were bleeding—badly—and her terror was palpable. Unless Fergus said otherwise, Ginny was needed where she was.

'You've cut your feet,' she told the little girl, making her voice sound astonished. She was trying to haul the child's attention from her mother to her feet. 'Goodness, what have you been doing?'

'I want Mummy,' the little girl sobbed, and Ginny's heart twisted. But this was hopeless. Fergus needed all his concentration if he was to get a good result, and there was no way the little girl could go to her mother.

So make a break and make it fast.

'Dr Fergus is looking after your mummy and I'm looking

after you,' she told the little one, forcing her voice to sound authoritative, hugging her close but standing and moving toward the door. 'We need to get bandages for your feet before you can come back and see Mummy.'

'Mummy.' The child's voice was a terrified scream.

Fergus looked up and met her eyes. He gave an imperceptible shake of his head.

Get her out of here, his body language said. Please.

'Let's go,' Ginny said. 'Bring what I need for stitching and dressing,' she told the nearest of the ambulance boys. 'Now.'

It took almost an hour to get the little girl's feet dressed. She sobbed and sobbed and in the end Ginny administered a sedative and then simply sat and hugged her close until the child's sobs subsided. Finally she collapsed into exhausted sleep and Ginny was able to lay her down on the bed in an empty ward and take care of the worst of the damage.

Some time while she'd hugged, the ambulance officer who'd brought her the dressings she'd needed had disappeared. Soon after he had been replaced by a young male nurse who'd introduced himself as Tony. Tony wasn't what Ginny was accustomed to in a nurse. Under his obviously hastily donned theatre gown, he was dressed in football gear—filthy shorts, a black and orange jersey, muddy socks and muddy knees. The six-foot-three footballer looked a mile away from a competent nurse, but his concern was genuine and when she started work she couldn't have asked for anyone better.

He helped clean the gravel from the worst of the cuts. It was painstaking work. Many of the stones were deeply embedded and when the feet were fully cleaned there were two cuts that needed stitches.

'Do we have any idea what happened?' Ginny asked as she stitched. Until the child had drifted into exhausted sleep she'd spoken only to her, but now there was space and time to talk to Tony.

'My beeper went off just at the final siren,' Tony told her.

'The groundskeeper gave me a ride in and he told me what he knows. The mother seems to have collapsed at the wheel of her car, half a mile or so from the football ground. Any houses close by would be empty. Everyone's at the footy. Maybe the mother told the kid to get help or maybe the kid figured that the source of noise was the only place to come. But they've just resurfaced the road. Gravel over bitumen. By the look of her feet, I'd reckon she must have run the whole way in bare feet.'

'That's what it looks like,' Ginny agreed, wincing in sympathy as she applied another piece of dressing over the stitched lacerations. 'Of all the brave…' She swallowed and looked down to the tear-stained little face. 'Do we know what's wrong with the mother?'

'Cardiomyopathy.' Fergus's frame was suddenly filling the open door, his face as bleak as death. 'And we've lost her.'

'Lost…' Ginny stared at him in consternation. She'd known. She'd seen it in the woman's face. 'But…'

'She went into cardiac arrest just as you left,' he said, and then, interpreting her distress, he put a hand out as if to ward off recriminations. 'There was nothing you could have done to help. Believe me, I'd have called you back if there was. We've been trying to figure out what went wrong and now we know.'

'Cardiomyopathy,' Ginny whispered, dazed. 'How on earth?'

'The local police sergeant's been through the car. There was a full medical history on the back seat. She must have travelled with it accessible—just in case. Plus she travelled with an oxygen supply. Plus enough medication to stock a small dispensary. She was desperately sick.'

'Then why on earth was she travelling?'

'Looking for one Richard Viental.' He hesitated, his eyes meeting hers and holding. 'Would that be…your Richard?'

'My Richard?' Ginny shook her head. 'I don't understand.'

'You think I do?' Fergus sounded weary, as if he'd taken in too much information for one man to absorb. As maybe he had. He'd lost a patient under his hands less than an hour ago—a young mother who by rights should have lived for another fifty years. No matter how long you were a doctor—did anyone ever get used to it?

'This letter was inserted as the first page of the medical history,' Fergus said, after a break while they all seemed to have trouble keeping breathing. Tony was winding leftover bandage, but after he finished he automatically started rewinding. Without the spool.

Fergus was holding a sheet of notepaper—a letter handwritten in a spidery hand that scrawled off the page.

'The police sergeant's read this,' he said, sounding apologetic and unsure. 'I've read it, too.' He sighed and looked down at the bed, where the little girl lay huddled in exhausted sleep. 'It's addressed to Richard but maybe you should read it as well,' he suggested.

'I… Should I phone Richard?' Ginny whispered, and he shook his head.

'Just read it.'

Dazed beyond belief, Ginny lifted the paper.

It was addressed to Richard. She shouldn't read it. But… She read.

Dear Richard.

I hope you don't have to read this. I hope I can tell you myself. Please God, I haven't left it too late. I've just kept on hoping, hoping…

By now you might hardly remember me. We were in hospital together, five years ago. You were in for check-ups after your lung transplant, just overnight for tests, and I remember being jealous. I was being assessed for a future heart transplant, and I thought wouldn't it be great to have it over. Like you had. But then the doctors told me I'd get another couple of years from my old heart. That's a laugh, isn't it? A couple of years… Five years and one baby later, it's still thumping. Just. Which is just as well, as there's no new heart for me.

Anyway, five years ago we were released from hospital

together. We went for a drink and I remember you looked great. I was feeling almost normal, high on the knowledge that I didn't have to face a transplant quite yet. Women were looking at me with you—and me thinking they looked jealous. Maybe I got a little bit drunk.

Maybe we both did.

The next day I was a bit worried about pregnancy. But I remember you laughing, bitter but laughing all the same, saying, 'No worries.' Sterility, you said. No kids ever, you said. I looked it up on the internet later, thinking you'd been lying, but you had grounds for thinking you were right. Ninety-eight per cent sterility, the article I read said for you.

Madison must be the result of the two per cent that got through.

Should I have told you?

Well, maybe I should, but by the time I realised I was pregnant I'd done more research on what I was facing and I guess I was…running? Everyone was saying I should have an abortion—put my health first, they said. I thought if you wanted me to have one as well I couldn't bear it. And I hardly knew you. You had so many plans—what to do with your new lungs. To tie you down with a sick woman…

No.

You know, maybe I thought that having Madison would kill me and maybe I even welcomed that.

Was that sick? Dumb? Maybe.

Anyway it didn't work. I made it through the pregnancy. Afterwards, when I realised what a wonderful thing we'd done—how special it is and how wonderful Madison is—I tried to ring you. But—your sister is it?—was at the address you gave me. She said you were back in hospital and there were problems with your transplant.

I hung up without telling her why I was calling. The last thing you needed was a daughter.

My mother said we'd be fine. My mother would always be there for Madison.

Only of course there's never a happy ending. Mum died last month of cancer and, what with the strain and everything, I had a cardiac arrest. They only just got me back and I'm on oxygen now and I know I'm failing. I shouldn't drive but…

I rang your apartment again—shades of desperation, huh?—and the caretaker told me you'd moved to the country. To your parents' farm. He gave me the address and I thought please let you be well, and even if you're not, you're at home with your parents, on a farm. A farm! Madison loves animals. Richard, she needs someone so much. I know I should see the social workers again and organise something for her and not hope for everything from you, but the last time I was ill she was in foster-care. It didn't work. She was so unhappy. I can't bear it.

Richard, you're her father. Please take care of your little girl.

If you get this letter it means….

I can't bear to think what it means.

Please love her to bits for me.

And thank you for giving me the gift of a daughter.

Yours with love—and with gratitude,

Judith Crammond

Ginny stared at the letter. She stared at it some more and the words blurred before her eyes.

'This can't be right,' she whispered at last, and Fergus hauled up a chair and sat beside her. He flicked a look up at Tony, and Tony gave an imperceptible nod and disappeared.

She was suddenly the patient, Ginny thought. She was about to be counselled.

'No,' she said blindly, and Fergus took the letter from her lifeless fingers, folded it carefully and put it on the bedside table.

'It seems crazy,' he said softly. 'But it seems that it's right. Judith was driving with a car full of medical paraphernalia. How she thought she was going to get here… Our local police sergeant, Ben Cross, has been in to see me. When Ben found the medical notes in the car, he rang the hospital on the letterhead to confirm we had the right woman. He brought the information straight in, thinking it might help.'

'It didn't,' she whispered.

'There was no way we could get her back,' Fergus continued, talking almost to himself. 'I couldn't believe what I was hearing when I put the stethoscope on her chest. I was waiting for her to arrest—I couldn't believe she hadn't done so already. Maybe it was just sheer willpower, to make sure her daughter was safe. Once she knew she was here she simply slipped away.'

'Her daughter was hardly safe,' Ginny whispered, and unconsciously her hand reached out to touch the little one's hair. This was…her brother's child? *Her niece?*

'The medical notes are from Sydney Central,' Fergus was saying. 'The hospital staff told Sergeant Cross there was no way Judith should be driving. They said she was far too sick. They've attempted to organise foster-care for the little girl but it's been refused. There are any number of their staff deeply concerned for the two of them.'

'Not enough to follow up.'

'There's only so much help you can force anyone to take,' Fergus said softly. 'This was Judith's little girl. She had to sort it out her own way.'

'She's sorted it out now?'

'I don't know,' Fergus said. 'Has she?'

'No.'

'This Richard. The man the note's addressed to.' He hesitated but then asked what he needed to know. 'He's your brother?'

'Yes.'

'Then would you like to tell me his side of the story? Or what you know of it.'

Ginny took a deep breath. And swallowed.

'Tell me, Ginny,' Fergus said, and he took her hand. It was one warm link in a world that had suddenly turned bewilderingly cold.

She had to tell him. She had to say it.

'Richard has cystic fibrosis,' she whispered at last. 'The lung transplant Judith talked about—yeah, it worked, but just for a while. Not for long enough. That's why we're here. That's why we're both here. This is where we were kids together. Richard's come home to die.'

There were medical imperatives to be got through.

Medicine had always been a retreat, Ginny thought as she moved on. Her studies and the resulting medical imperatives had been the means to block off the reality of the outside world for a long time, and they helped her now.

Oscar had to be got to bed.

'Though the way you have him wedged, he's safer on his door,' Tony said admiringly, and Ginny even managed a smile. Oscar was deeply asleep, snoring so loudly the glass Tony had set on the bedside table was vibrating. The Ventolin was taking effect. His breathing was easier and there was no trace of pain on his face as he slept.

'I guess this gets to be our happy ending for the afternoon,' Ginny told Tony, trying to make her voice sound normal.

'We need one.' Tony looked at her fingers as she tried to adjust the drip rate and suddenly the big nurse was moving to take the equipment away from her. Her fingers were shaking and she couldn't do a damned thing about it.

So much for burying herself in medical imperatives.

'I can manage here,' he told her. 'You've done enough, Dr Viental. Go find Dr Reynard.' Then he smiled, a great footballer's smile that totally enveloped his face. Pushing her to cheer up. 'Hey, we've gone from a tiny nursing home with no doctors to two doctors on staff. How great is that?'

'I'm not on staff.'

'You look like you're on staff from here,' he told her. But then his smile died. 'Ginny, I know about your family. I'm so—'

'Leave it,' she said roughly.

'Go and find Fergus,' he said gently. 'Go and do what needs to be done.'

Fergus was making phone calls. Ginny found him in the office marked 'Medical Director', though the letters were faded and the 'D' looked more like a 'C'. He was talking to someone about what had just happened.

Ginny entered the room, leaned against the wall and waited for him to finish. She felt drained of all energy. Where to go to from here?

'I'm not sure whether we need a social worker or not,' Fergus was saying into the phone. 'For tonight we'll keep her in hospital. But there's family here.'

Family. That would be...her?

Richard was supposed to be the end, she thought. The end of family for ever. How could she keep giving?

She couldn't.

Fergus replaced the receiver and looked at her. For a moment nothing was said. He simply...looked.

Clear grey eyes, calmly assessing. Maybe seeing more than she wanted him to see.

'We need to talk to Richard,' he said. 'How sick is he?'

'He's really sick. We can't tell him this.'

'Why not?'

'He's dying,' she said desperately. 'How do you think it'll make him feel?'

'If you were dying, would you want to know you had a daughter?'

'No! It'd complicate my life.'

'But it's part of life, and an important part,' Fergus said gently. 'Richard's not dead yet. Is he mentally impaired?'

'No.'

'Then he has the right to be treated as alive while he is alive. He has to know.'

'Oh, God, how can I tell him?'

'Let me do it for you.'

She stiffened, trying to protect herself with anger. 'I don't need you to tell me how to treat my own brother.'

'I'm not telling you how to treat him. I'm offering to help.'

Anger wasn't going to work. So what was new? She paused and tried to think what to say.

Nothing came.

Helplessly she crossed to the window, staring down through the bushland to the lake beyond. Most of the buildings in this valley were built to face the lake. The lake itself was teardrop-shaped, a couple of miles across, blue and glistening in the ring of dense bushland around it.

Cradle Lake.

When she had been small, she and her family had spent every summer's day they could manage on this lake. They'd swum, they'd built moats on the shore, they'd had fun. She had a glistening memory as a six-year-old, of swimming triumphantly from the shore to the buoy marking the start of deep water. It had been her first real swim. She remembered turning to see her father with nine-year-old Richard cheering her on. Her mother, with toddler Chris in the shallows, was clapping and laughing as well, then yelling at them to come and get their picnic tea.

It was her last good memory.

Richard had taken longer than most cystic fibrosis sufferers to get dangerously ill. He'd had bowel problems as a baby, and infection after infection during childhood, but the diagnosis hadn't been picked up. Chris had become bad first, diagnosed soon after that day at the lake, their local doctor finally coming up with the answer. One sibling sick had meant there was a likelihood more could be. So Richard's diagnosis had been made as well, and Ginny's parents had been advised to have no more children.

But, of course, Toby had already been on the way. There had been no going back.

Richard was the last of her family. The end. Finished.

But...

'This means I'll have family again,' she whispered to the lake.

'You don't want family?'

'I've had family. Parents. Three brothers.'

'And?'

'Chris died when he was eight. Toby died when he was ten. My father disappeared. After Chris's death, when it seemed Toby would soon follow, he simply walked out and never came back. Then after Toby's death my mother drank herself into oblivion.'

His face didn't change. 'Leaving you.'

'To what was left of my family,' she whispered. 'But that's finished and now you'll make me take on Madison.'

'No one's making you take on anyone.'

'Are you kidding?' She whirled on him, furious. 'You've seen her. She's Richard's daughter. She even looks like us. When I saw her… She looks familiar and it's how they all looked. My little brothers. Chris and then Toby. Do you know what sort of a childhood I had? I was six when it all started to fall apart and I've nursed them all since. And now… You'll tell Richard he has a daughter and he'll accept her—of course he'll accept her—and of course he won't ask me to take her on. He knows how much it'll hurt. But he doesn't have to ask. He'll just look at her and it'll be done.'

'Maybe it's already done,' he said gently. 'Maybe it was done from the time she was conceived. You just didn't know about it until now.'

'Have you any idea how much it hurts?' Her voice cracked on a sob. She swallowed it and made herself continue. 'You sit there and you have no idea…no idea at all. What you're asking me to do.'

'Ginny, she's not your daughter.' He hadn't moved. It was like he was locked into position. 'You can arrange foster-care or adoption for her after Richard dies, or there might be other family on Judith's side who you can give her to.'

'Oh, sure.'

'You can, Ginny,' he said softly. 'It's possible to walk away.'

'How the hell would you know?'

'I've watched it done. It's possible to stay detached.'

'Yeah, and go crazy.'

'You need to keep things in perspective.'

'There's no perspective,' she flung at him. 'I don't want this.'

'So walk away now.' He was watching her dispassionately, his voice curiously calm. 'This is Richard's daughter. Not yours. He may be dying but he has the right to sort things out. He has no right to include you in those plans.'

'As if he couldn't. As soon as he knows of her existence, then she's part of my family. Part of my responsibility. He mustn't... He mustn't.'

'You're suggesting we don't tell him?' He rose, circling the desk to join her at the window.

'I don't know what to suggest,' she said, and her voice was dull, bleak and accepting already that what she wanted had little to do with the way things would pan out. 'I can't do this. I've had enough.'

'You're tired of caring?'

'I want out. I don't want to love anything, anyone, ever again.' Her voice trailed off and she lifted her hands to her face, hiding...hiding from what?

There was no place to hide. She knew it and so did Fergus.

He took her hands in his, drawing them down, gripping them with a warmth and strength that said he knew what she was going through. That he understood.

Which was an illusion. No one knew what she was going through. She didn't understand it herself.

'You just do what comes next,' he said softly, drawing her in and hugging her. She felt herself be drawn. She had no strength to fight him.

She'd been fighting to be solitary for so long—to stay aloof. Richard's death was to be the final step in her path to independence.

She didn't need this man to hug her. She didn't need anyone.

But she didn't fight him. For this moment she needed him too much. Human contact. That was all it was, she thought fiercely. Warmth and strength and reassurance. It was an illusion, she knew, but for now...

For now she let herself be held. She let her body melt against his, letting him take a weight that had suddenly seemed unbearable. He was strong and firm and warm. His lips were touching her hair.

She should pull away, but she couldn't. For now she needed this too much.

No one had held her like this. Not ever, she thought. Or maybe…maybe when she had been tiny, when she'd still been a child, when she hadn't had the weight of the family firmly on her shoulders.

Had her parents ever held her like this? They must have, but that had been so long ago that she'd forgotten.

'I don't do…relationships,' she muttered, and his hands shifted so he was holding her by the waist.

'Good. Neither do I.'

'You're holding me.'

'It's a medical massage,' he said, and she heard a lazy smile in his voice. 'When all else fails—hug.'

She liked it, she decided. In times of crisis—hug?

Who was she kidding? You needed someone to be permanent to hug, and people weren't permanent. You needed to let yourself close to find that degree of security but with that closeness came…peril.

If she lost anyone else…

'Don't do it,' she whispered. 'I'm not getting close to you, Fergus Reynard.'

'I think you already are,' he said, chuckling and holding her closer. 'But I know what you mean. You needn't worry. This is for now, because I suspect it's what we both need. But it's only for now. I'm here for twelve weeks and then I'm out of here.'

'Why did you come?'

'Maybe I knew how much I was needed,' he told her, but she could tell by the tone in his voice that it was much more than that.

'You're running,' she said, and he shook his head and put her away from him. She looked into his face and what she saw there…

This was no young medic taking a locum job to save for the next overseas jaunt, she thought. There was a recognition here…

Theirs was a shared journey, she realised bleakly. She didn't know the details but she knew she was right, and she also knew… What he said was the truth. He could hold her as much as she needed but there was no fear of further commitment. She'd built her fences and so had he.

Two levels of razor wire around their hearts. Maybe his was impervious. She'd thought hers was, too, but out there…

Out there in the ward was a little girl called Madison, and the only way for her to survive was for Ginny's barriers to come down.

No. There must be some other way.

'Madison will sleep for hours,' Fergus said softly into her hair. 'Miriam and Tony will care for her. Oscar's stable and there are no other patients in this place except nursing-home residents. Can I take you home to meet Richard?'

'I need to tell him…'

'We need to tell him nothing,' Fergus said. 'Judith has written to him. We give him the letter and we help him sort out what he wants done.'

'Dear God…'

'There's no way through this but through this,' Fergus told her. 'Let's do it.'

CHAPTER FOUR

RICHARD had been sleeping when Ginny had left him.

The back veranda of the old farmhouse looked down over the lake, facing west so afternoon sun drenched the ancient sofas and rickety chairs left over from when they'd lived here. This had been their favourite place as children, and it was their favourite place now. Richard had fought every inch of the way with this disease but in the last couple of weeks his fighting had ceased. He wanted to see no one but Ginny. 'I'm closing my world down,' he'd told Ginny when she'd had to turn away requests from old friends to see him. 'I'm severing ties.' He'd slept more and more, and out on the veranda Ginny had found some measure of peace.

What she had to do now… What she had to tell him…

Severing ties? Ha!

But Fergus was right behind her, and his presence helped a little. It made the impossible seem possible—just. She climbed the veranda steps and turned to where they'd organised Richard's daybed.

The bed was empty.

Why? Richard had trouble moving. She'd left him set up with everything he needed, but if he'd had to go to the bathroom… Had he fallen?

Abandoning Fergus, she hauled the screen door open and headed inside. 'Richard?' she called. 'Richard?'

Nothing.

He wasn't in his bedroom, but he hardly used his bedroom, preferring to sleep where he could watch the stars. He wasn't in the bathroom or in the kitchen.

She came back out to the veranda at a run, concern deepening to fear.

The bedclothes were flung back as if he'd just left. He'd had his oxygen cylinder on a trolley, so he could tug it with him if he needed to. It was gone.

'What's wrong?' Fergus asked but she ignored him.

'Richard?'

And then she saw her car.

It was at the far side of the house to where Fergus had driven in. It was a small red sedan, a bit battered and not particularly noticeable. But it was noticeable now.

There was a garden hose snaking into the driver's side window, and rags wedging the rest of the gap closed. Richard's oxygen cylinder was lying on its side, abandoned beside the driver's side door.

'Richard,' she screamed, but Fergus was before her. He'd seen. He was down the veranda steps, crossing to the car in huge strides, hauling the car door open.

Richard was slumped at the wheel. As Fergus pulled open the door, he toppled sideways.

He would have fallen right out, but Fergus held him. He crouched and caught him, breaking his fall, hauling him free from the car in the one swift movement.

Ginny's hands were on his neck, feeling for a pulse, feeling…

There was one. She had a pulse. Thready, but a pulse nevertheless.

'He's breathing,' Fergus said, and her world somehow started up again from a dead stop.

'Richard,' she whispered. 'Richard.'

He opened his eyes and stared at her. He even managed a sickly smile.

'Richard,' she said again, brokenly, fighting nausea.

'You could,' her brother said softly, his voice the thread of a weary whisper, 'have filled the bloody thing up with petrol.'

* * *

Fergus carried him back to bed.

Once Richard had been too heavy to carry. The cystic fibrosis which had killed her younger brothers early had been gentler with him, slower in its deadly progress. He'd had a time when he'd almost seemed normal—when his body had almost seemed as if it could be healthy.

That time was long past. Her good-looking, vibrant brother was now an emaciated thread of a man, close to death.

That afternoon he'd come within a hair's breadth. Ginny trailed behind Fergus, carrying Richard's oxygen, still trying to fight down the waves of sickness.

She shouldn't have left him. She'd wanted a walk. Then, when she'd stopped in on the way to the hospital, he'd seemed fine.

'Go,' he'd said. 'Go be a ministering angel to someone else for a change and let me enjoy the sunset.'

She faltered as she reached the stop step of the veranda and Fergus set Richard on his bed and glanced back at her. 'He's fine,' he told her as she set the oxygen tank down. 'Richard's fine.'

She wasn't. She needed the bathroom. Fast.

When she came out Richard was settled back on his pillows, attached again to oxygen. He looked even paler than usual, but his chest was rising and falling with reassuring rhythm.

The sight of him made the nausea return. Ginny plonked herself down on the back step and stuck her head between her knees.

'See what you've done to your sister?' Fergus said mildly, and Richard grimaced.

'She did it to me,' he whispered. 'Hell, Ginny, I just assumed...'

'That I had a full tank,' she managed.

'I didn't even look. A few minutes, then splutter, splutter... I couldn't believe it. All that trouble.'

'So is life that bad for you? That you want to finish what's left of it now?' Fergus's voice was nothing but conversational.

Ginny was staring down over the lake, trying to control the shudders that threatened to be her undoing. She felt sick to the soul. Too much had happened too fast and her mind was having trouble catching up with her stomach.

But Richard was alive. That was all that mattered for now, she told herself. Everything else could take care of itself at some future time.

'Who the hell are you?' Richard was asking, and she tried to focus enough to listen.

'I'm a doctor, mate,' Fergus said. 'Fergus Reynard. I brought your sister home.'

'I'm supposed to say thank you?'

'We didn't save your life, if that's what you're suggesting,' Fergus said mildly. 'Seems Ginny did that by being lousy with her petrol buying.'

'I was going to fill it up yesterday,' Ginny whispered. 'But it was raining. I thought there was enough to get into town again tomorrow, and the weather'd be better.'

But neither man seemed to be listening to her.

Maybe she wasn't listening to herself.

'So why did you decide topping yourself was a good idea?' Fergus asked.

'Is that any of your business?'

'I imagine it's your sister's, and I think Ginny's past asking.'

'Leave us be,' Richard said wearily, sinking into his pillows. 'It doesn't matter.'

'I'm guessing it does. To Ginny as well as to you.'

'I'm dying anyway.'

'Are you scared, then?' Fergus asked. 'Of what's to come?'

'No.'

'Then why?'

'Ginny's stuck here,' he managed, and took a few gasping breaths of oxygen while Ginny took that on board.

'You think I mind that?' she demanded. 'You think I resent spending a few weeks of my life with you? Richard...' She broke off, unable to go on.

'You've done this so often,' Richard muttered. He swivelled

a little so he was staring at Fergus, and his eyes were almost fierce. 'I had two kid brothers with this damned disease. My father sloped off and our mother coped via the bottle. She died of cirrhosis of the liver when Ginny was sixteen. Ginny's done the lot.'

'You've been there, too,' Ginny whispered, and her voice broke.

'You know that's a lie, and I won't be with you for this one,' Richard whispered, and closed his eyes. 'You'll be alone. When I thought there was time this afternoon...'

'You'd just get it over with,' Fergus ended for him.

'What else is there to live for?'

There was a deathly silence. It went on and on. Maybe Fergus was waiting for her to say something, Ginny thought, but she couldn't. She couldn't.

'As it happens,' Fergus said finally, still with the friendly, interested tone about him, 'there is something you might like to live a bit longer for. If you're not afraid.'

'I'm not afraid.'

'That's sensible. I'm not sure who looked after your brothers while they died, or what sort of deaths they had, but I'm here to tell you that if you permit me I can take care of you for as long as you want. I can keep you absolutely comfortable. I can keep it so you're in control, every step of the way. No decision will be made without your say-so. Short of helping you into gas-filled cars, you'll find that medical help can make the next few weeks as fulfilling as you want them to be.'

'As fulfilling?' Richard said. 'Drifting into white wings and halos?'

'There's some who reckon it's hosts of virgins,' Fergus said mildly, and grinned. 'Me, I don't know, but even with virgins waiting upstairs, peacefully slipping away seems like you're dead already. Which, thanks to Ginny's lousiness with the petrol, now isn't true. You're alive until you're dead, mate. You're not dead yet and you have a job to do.'

'Which is?' Richard sounded stunned. As well he might, Ginny thought. She was feeling pretty stunned herself.

'Getting to know your daughter,' Fergus said bluntly, and handed him Judith's letter.

Afterwards they walked out to the car together.

Richard had taken in the contents of the letter, had asked incredulous questions—and then had suddenly slept. It was as if the culminating emotions of the day had simply become overwhelming and his body had demanded time out.

There had been no denial, however. Simply a barrage of questions, then silence, then sleep.

Silence seemed good. Ginny walked Fergus back to his car and silence seemed the only option.

'If I leave you, promise you won't commit suicide yourself,' Fergus asked as he reached the driver's door.

'Not enough petrol,' she said, and gave a short laugh. Which almost turned into a sob. Almost but not quite. She managed to haul herself back together but it took an effort.

'Ginny, this is a—'

'There's no need to swear,' she broke in. 'I know exactly what it is.'

His hand reached out and took hers. It was a strong grasp, warm and reassuring. It was his bedside manner, she thought, and she was suddenly angry. She might as well be angry as anything else, she thought, and tried to haul her hand away.

He didn't release it.

'I'm fine,' she said unnecessarily, but still he didn't release it.

'You're not fine,' he said softly. 'You were sick back there.'

'Reaction.'

'Of course it was reaction. How long have you been with Richard?'

'This time?'

'This time,' he said, and his face grew a little grim, hearing the years of commitment behind those two words.

'Since he came out of hospital. They wanted to move him into a hospice but it was better that he came back here.'

'Better for who?'

'I've learned the hard way,' she said softly, 'that it's easier to do what's asked rather than live with regrets afterwards.'

'So it's as hard as I think it is, coming back here?'

Her eyes flew to his. With shock. He knew.

'I…'

'Did your brothers die here?' he asked. 'And your mother? I'm thinking you'd never want to be back here.'

Silence.

'You were here for them?'

More silence.

'And Richard? Was Richard there when the rest of your family died? Did you have any support?'

'Richard's been ill,' she said defensively, and she knew by the look on his face that he understood the story behind that, too. Or part of it. Richard hadn't wanted to spend his limited life caring for dying siblings or distraught parents. He'd turned off at an early age, making every excuse to be away from home.

Ginny didn't blame him. He had been ill and young, and the fact that she'd been given no choice didn't mean she had to resent Richard.

'Let's think of a plan here,' Fergus said, and she managed to haul her hand from his and glare.

'There's no plan.'

'There has to be,' he said. 'I'll come back after evening clinic and see what Richard has decided to do.'

'Richard won't decide to do anything.'

'He must.'

'You can't put the responsibility for—'

'For his daughter on him?' All of a sudden Fergus sounded grim, sympathy fading. 'Yes, I can. But it's not me doing it. Like it or not, this little one is his daughter and, no matter how sick he is, he needs to face that. Sure he's shocked…'

'Fergus, this afternoon he tried to kill himself.'

'Did he?' He looked down at her, and she could no longer read his face. 'You know, even a dying man can read a fuel gauge, Ginny.'

She gasped. 'What are you saying? He wouldn't have staged it. What possible reason—?'

'I suspect he's wanting more help than he thinks you're prepared to give.'

She didn't understand. 'He knows I'm prepared to give whatever's needed. He refused to go to a hospice and he asked me to be here for him. I said I would and I will.'

'Which fits with my theory,' Fergus said evenly. 'Why go to all this trouble to come back here if just to kill himself? If he'd really wanted to die he could have killed himself back in the city. Why come here?'

'I don't have a clue. But it's taken me so much work to get this place back into habitable state. To organise equipment here…'

'That's what I mean. Ginny, what would you have done just now if I hadn't been here?'

'Exactly the same as if you had. Pulled him out. Got him back to bed. Been sick.'

'And not left him alone again,' he said gently. 'Tomorrow…you're not going to leave him for more than a few minutes, are you?'

'I… How can I?'

'Which means he's got what he needs. He's asked you to come back here and you've come. This afternoon you were away for several hours and I suspect he hated it and it made him fearful. Now he's fixed it so that you can't leave him. It's called emotional blackmail, Ginny, and you need to see it for what it is. We need to organise you some help.'

She stared at him, incredulous. 'I don't need help.'

'You do,' he said, and smiled.

Which made her insides twist. Why did his smile affect her like this? she wondered wildly. She shouldn't be emotional. She mustn't be. She'd been through too much in the past to fall to bits now.

'I can cope,' she muttered.

'Sure you can. But you needn't.' He glanced at his watch

and grimaced. 'I have patients waiting. I need to go. But expect me back at eight tonight.'

'I don't want you back.'

'Sure you do,' he said, and grinned. 'You and your brother both need me and, like Batman, I always turn up when I'm needed. When the world needs saving.'

'Wearing your jocks on the outside?' she managed, bewildered, and he smiled.

'That's better,' he told her. 'Much better.' Then, before she could guess what he was about to do, he lifted his palm to her cheek. His hand rested against her face—just for a moment. It was a gesture of warmth and strength and solidarity. It was a gesture that said she wasn't alone.

She didn't need such a gesture. She didn't.

She backed away from him, and he let her go.

But then, as his car drove out of the driveway, as he headed off back to his medicine, back to his hospital, back to his outside world, her hand came up to retrace the path of his fingers.

There was still warmth there.

She didn't need help.

But she stood and held her hand against her face for a very long time.

Richard slept. He woke briefly to eat the dinner Ginny prepared but he said little.

'I don't want to talk about it,' he said when Ginny raised the matter of the letter, and when he saw she intended to push he simply turned back over on his pillows and slept some more.

How could you hit a dying man? She couldn't. But the flare of anger behind her panic refused to disappear completely.

It was all very well for him, cocooned in his pillows, knowing he was leaving, accepting that any problems were hers and not his.

Emotional blackmail? Maybe.

She washed up, went outside and stared down at the lake. The sun set late here. It was still a tangerine ball behind low-lying clouds on the horizon.

It was an hour before Fergus was due back.

If she left and Richard woke up...

She walked across to his bed and stared down at him. Fergus's words came back to her. *Even a dying man can read a fuel gauge.*

He wasn't dying this week. He'd survived petrol fumes and fear without his oxygen.

'You're alive until you're dead,' she said softly, not knowing whether he could hear her or not but not really caring. 'Richard, don't do this to me.'

Silence.

Of course there was silence.

What to do?

There was no television in this place. No radio. It was all very well staring out over the lake until you die, she thought bleakly but she wasn't dying.

She actually felt ever so slightly more alive at the moment than she'd felt for a while.

Was that something to do with a pair of caring grey eyes and the touch of fingers against her face?

Oh, yeah, let's fall in love with the doctor, shall we? she said to herself, mocking. She'd do no such thing.

She very carefully kept herself free of relationships and Fergus was no exception. This feeling she had was nonsense.

She should sit and watch the sunset.

She stared at the sunset for three or four minutes. It was a very nice sunset.

Enough.

She turned back to the bed, to her sleeping brother.

'I'm going over to Oscar's to check his lambs and make sure his dogs have been fed,' she told his non-responsive form. 'I'll be back in three-quarters of an hour. Don't die while I'm away.' She bit her lip and then added, 'And if you do, it's not my fault.'

CHAPTER FIVE

OSCAR should never have been permitted to farm. She should never have agreed to let him use their land to graze his cattle. She knew that as she trudged back over the paddocks. It was yet another burden on her heart, but at least the walk over the hills got a bit of air into her lungs and gave her a chance to take a little time out from the impossibility of what lay ahead.

And at first it seemed things were OK. Ginny checked the house paddock where she'd left her lamb who'd been stuck in the cattle grid. Everything there was great. The sheep there were surrounding the trough, as if not brave enough to leave it in case it drained again. Her rescued lamb was suckling from his resigned mother, his tiny tail wagging with the ferocious intensity of an avid eater.

One happy ending. Great.

She walked back behind the house, up to the paddock where Oscar kept his lambing ewes. She'd been there earlier that afternoon and had found six sad mounds of disintegrating wool, stories of lambing gone wrong.

There were ewes and lambs everywhere here. Lambing was almost at an end. She ran her eyes over the flock. Searching for trouble.

And, of course, she found it. There was one ewe down.

Why had she looked for trouble? she demanded of herself. Oscar had left his flock to their fate, letting nature take its course. So should she.

She couldn't. She walked over and knelt by the ewe. The animal had gone past straining, lying on her side and panting, gazing ahead with eyes that were starting to dull with pain.

'I'm not an obstetrician,' she told the sheep, but she checked what was happening and winced. 'Ouch.'

She couldn't leave her. A bucket of hot soapy water might help Very soapy water. And a bit of luck…

She rose and Fergus was standing by the paddock gate, watching her.

'Medical emergency,' she said briefly, and walked across to meet him. He held the gate open for her and she passed him, aware that she smelt like sheep again and he didn't. Aware that he was six inches taller than her. Aware that he had great eyes…

'I didn't think you'd leave Richard,' he said.

'I seem to remember you told me I might,' she said. 'Plus he's sleeping. Plus we've run out of petrol. Why are you here?'

'Same as you, I'd imagine. I thought I'd check on our lamb.'

Our lamb. It had a nice ring to it, she thought. A glimmer of humour in a day that had been singularly without any such thing.

'He's fine.'

'So I see. But there's a ewe in trouble?'

'The lamb's stuck. One foot out, nothing else. I need to find some lubricant.'

'What's your medical speciality?' he called after her. She'd hardly stopped walking. He closed the gate behind her and now he caught her up as she headed into the house.

'Emergency medicine,' she said briefly. 'Yours?'

'I'm a surgeon.'

A surgeon. What was a surgeon doing in Cradle Lake?

No matter. Concentrate on the job at hand.

'So if neither of us is an obstetrician… You reckon between us we can deliver a lamb?'

'I reckon between us we can call a vet.'

'No time,' she said over her shoulder, reaching the ramp up to the veranda and shoving her way past interested dogs. 'The vet comes from Marlborough and the ewe will be dead by then. She's young. Too damned young to have been joined, I'd have said, but, then, I'm a doctor, not a farmer.'

'You spent your childhood here?'

'Yeah.'

'So you farmed.'

'So I did.' They were through Oscar's back door. She grabbed a bucket by the laundry trough and started running hot water. 'Can you find a sheet or something that I can rip up to make a rope?'

'How about a rope?'

'Too coarse. I don't want to deliver a lamb only to put it down because I've damaged it.'

'You think it's still alive?'

'I didn't listen for foetal heartbeat if that's what you mean,' she said, exasperated. 'Dr Reynard, do you want to be some use?'

'I... Yes.'

'Then go find a sheet and join me out there.'

When Fergus got back to the paddock, Ginny was lying full length in the mud.

'Why do ewes never choose a nice soft grassy patch to give birth?' she muttered as he approached. 'What is it with the muddiest, hardest, rockiest spot in the paddock? Ow!'

'Ow?' he said cautiously, and knelt to watch what she was doing.

She was trying to manipulate...

'The shoulder's stuck,' she said tightly. 'One foot's come free and not the other. I need to get it back in and get the two legs out together. If that happens, maybe I can get it's head down. Only she's having contractions again.'

She was. Maybe it was their presence, but the ewe had finally decided to come to life again. Her belly was rippling with strong contractions and she was even struggling to rise.

Here was something he could do. He pressed the sheep's head down with one hand and laid his other hand firmly on her flank.

'It's OK, girl,' he told the ewe softly. 'Dr Viental's an emergency specialist. You couldn't be in better hands.'

Ginny cast him a suspicious glance and kept on working. She had small hands, he thought, which was just as well. She was using the soap as lubricant, trying to manoeuvre in the birth canal. Which was just a bit tricky when the contractions were designed to push her hand out again.

'Can you tell her not to push?' she gasped.

'Don't push,' he told the ewe. 'Remember your breathing techniques.'

The ewe had obviously forgotten.

Ginny swore again. The force of the contraction would be crushing her fingers. Then: 'Got it,' she said, and at the next contraction another tiny hoof appeared.

Two hooves.

'Tie them,' she told him, swivelling to soap her hands again. 'Just tight enough to give you some purchase. It's almost impossible to pull by hand.'

'We're going to pull?'

'When I get the head in position. Breathe, damn you,' she told the ewe. 'If you push now, you'll risk breaking your baby's neck.'

Her fingers were already working, using the break in contractions to find purchase.

Fergus was looping the sheet, twisting it so the two little hooves were tied together, with a little of the sheet folded between them so they didn't crush each other. His fingers were right against Ginny's. There was so little room.

Another contraction and she grunted in pain.

'Not yet,' she muttered. 'I can't… I can't… Yes!'

'Yes?' Fergus said, cautious.

'Head's down. Next contraction I want you to pull, very gently. I'll leave my fingers where they are, pushing the head down.'

He looked at how far inside the ewe her hand was. He remembered the strength of the contraction. 'Your fingers are behind the head. You'll break something.'

'I won't break anything,' she told him. 'I'm tough as old boots. But I may just swear.'

'I won't listen.'

'Very wise,' she muttered, and he didn't listen—or not very much—and one minute later a feeble excuse for a lamb slithered out into Fergus's waiting hands.

It was alive.

Some things were instinctive. Newborn lambs weren't so different from newborn human babies and he'd done his basic med training in obstetrics. Almost as soon as it was out, he was clearing its nose, checking its airways, making sure...

It gave a pathetic, mewing attempt at a bleat and Ginny grinned.

'We have lift-off, Houston?'

'Indeed we do,' Fergus said, wiping the lamb on what was left of Oscar's bed sheet. This felt good, he thought. More. Somehow in the drama of this day they'd been granted a little happy ending.

Two happy endings, he thought, if they counted the lamb they'd pulled from the cattle grid.

The ewe's head was turned. She was straining to see, and Fergus lifted the tiny creature round to its mother's head.

'Well done, us,' Ginny whispered, and wiped her face with the back of her hand.

Which maybe wasn't such a good idea.

'You look like you've just been playing with a chainsaw,' Fergus told her, and she grinned, knowing he was feeling exactly the same as she was. Deaths while practising medicine were unavoidable. There was nothing like an intervention and a saved life to balance things up.

It didn't make it better but it helped get things in perspective. A bit.

'What's a bit of blood between friends?' she demanded, and he grinned back at her, enjoying her pleasure.

'You love your medicine?'

'I do indeed.' She rose, tossing soap and scraps of linen into her bucket. 'It takes me into another place.'

'As opposed to the place you're stuck in.'

Her smile faded. 'Leave it,' she said. She stood, looking down at ewe and lamb. The lamb was nuzzling the ewe's flank, already searching for a teat. The ewe was still down but she was starting to move.

There was a warm night in front of them. She'd be safe. She'd make it.

'We have another baby to care for now,' Fergus said gently and she flinched.

'Madison?'

'Madison.'

'I don't know how to face it,' she said bluntly, and he nodded.

'That's what I'm here for.'

'So we're out in the paddock, delivering lambs.'

He smiled, a gentle smile that said he knew how she was feeling. It was a false smile, she thought. How could he know? But somehow it worked.

He was a doctor with an excellent bedside manner, she decided, trying to get a hold on things that were impossible to get a hold on.

Ginny hadn't been near Cradle Lake since her mother had died. The house had been rented out for years. It had taken a huge amount of effort—and money—to get it to the stage where she could take care of Richard there. And now, standing in the paddocks looking down over the lake, with emotions surging through her that had been in overdrive since the first of her brothers had been diagnosed...

This man wasn't helping, she thought. She'd fought since she'd been a kid to get some form of emotional independence. Not to break apart when she lost things.

Now, suddenly, she wanted to fall on this guy's chest and weep—and what use would that be to anybody?

'You met Tony? Our footballer-cum-nurse?' Fergus was asking.

'Yes.'

'He's out at your house right now,' Fergus told her. 'He's talking things through with Richard. It seems he and Richard were in the same grade at school here, and Tony says they were friends. Tony reckons he can help.'

'No one can help and Richard doesn't want anyone,' she snapped before she could stop herself, but he appeared not to notice her anger.

'Cradle Lake's a tiny community,' he said. 'They're geared to help.'

'They haven't in the past. You heard Oscar.'

'Yeah, I talked to Tony about that,' he said thoughtfully. He had his hands in his pockets and was watching the newborn lamb suckle her mother. The ewe had struggled to her feet. It seemed that maybe life was going to go on after all.

'It seems your parents pretty much drove the community away,' he said, and she flinched. 'Like Richard's doing now.'

'My dad left us when Chris died.'

'And your mother hit the bottle and kept the community away. You cared for her alone, and for Toby until he died. Any time someone came near they were hit with abuse. In the end, when there was no one left but you, you were left to social workers.'

Ginny didn't say anything in response to that. She remembered that time, though. Just after Toby's death…

Richard had been eighteen then, and he hadn't even stuck around for the funeral. He had been ill, but not so ill he had been unable to manage to care for himself. He'd had a girl-friend, and they'd simply climbed into his girlfriend's combi-van and headed for Queensland.

'I'll look after him,' Ginny remembered the girl telling her. 'The weather up there will be better for his lungs and this way you don't have to look after him as well.'

Ginny had been fifteen. Toby had been two days dead.

Her mother had been comatose.

That had been when Social Security had stepped in. Ginny had been placed with a foster-family in Sydney—great people who'd helped her get where she'd most wanted to be.

Which was independent.

She had been independent, until the disease had finally caught up with Richard, as they'd always known it would.

And now…

'Tony's taken bedding out to your place,' Fergus said softly, watching her face. 'In case Richard decides he wants to keep Madison close.'

'I can't take care of Madison,' she said, panicked.

'No one's asking you to, Ginny,' Fergus said gently. 'There was a bit of a community meeting this afternoon. People wanted to help your family twenty years ago and they weren't permitted to. Oscar's the exception rather than the rule. Cradle Lake was horrified at what happened to you, and everyone really wants to help. If you'll permit…'

'If I'll permit?'

'It has to be your decision,' he told her. 'Or some of it does. Whether Richard wants to be a part of Madison's life, for whatever time he has left, is up to him, but the rest… If he does want to spend time with his daughter, then Miriam will come out here later tonight. She'll bring Madison with her. And she and Tony will take turns to stay as a live-in nurse to the pair of them. For as long as it takes. I know Richard doesn't want anyone but he hasn't a choice in this, Ginny. We've organised it to care for you and if he doesn't want it…well, there's still the hospice in Sydney.' He smiled. 'But I think you'll find Tony's persuaded him. He can be very persuasive, our Tony. Best goal-kicker in the district and there's a reason.'

His smile was persuading her to join him but she couldn't. It was as if all the air had been sucked out of her lungs, leaving her with nothing.

'Well?' he said softly, and her eyes flew to his. His gaze was gentle, questioning, expecting an answer.

'Tony's telling Richard that he has no choice,' he continued gently. 'He's telling him that what he's asked you to do is too hard, and the community as a whole has decided to share. You nursed your little brothers until they died and you nursed your mother. Your mother drove the community away but they won't stand back this time and do nothing.'

'They can't do anything else.'

'That's what you think,' he told her. 'You have no idea. No one knew that the new people in the Viental place were Vientals, or there'd have been neighbours round here by now.' His smile deepened. 'You have no concept of the network in this valley. I've been here a few days and already I know that the community network is just plain scary. Casserole production has gone into overdrive. There are even farmers offering to take over livestock duty on this place—not because they like Oscar but because they know you, and they've already guessed that you won't be able to leave Oscar's stock to fend for themselves.'

She swallowed. 'I don't... I can't... Madison...'

'There are two things that can happen with Madison,' he told her, his voice calmly reassuring. 'There's no need to look like a startled rabbit, because we've talked about that, too.'

'We?'

'Me and Tony and Miriam and a number of locals who I bet you can hardly remember but who clearly remember you. The idea is to give you some space. Depending on what Richard wants tonight, there are different courses of action. If he wants her now, then we'll bring her out here. Miriam and Tony will stay and we'll nurse her back to health alongside her father.' He hesitated. 'It seems hard, introducing a child to a father who hasn't long to live, but, Ginny, Madison's almost five years old. I remember a bit of what happened when I was that old, and I bet you do, too. You don't remember much, but some things stick. We think that maybe it's more important that Madison be left with a shadowy remembrance of a father than no remembrance at all.'

His voice faltered. She stared up at him. There was suddenly pain in his face.

Pain for Madison?

No. He had his own shadows, she realised. There was a reason he was here.

'Why—?'

'Not now,' he said, and she knew he'd sensed the question

that was forming. Somehow he seemed to read her mind before she even knew what she was thinking herself. 'For now, all you need to think is that Madison is Richard's daughter. Not yours. There's no reason why the burden of raising her has to rest on your shoulders. There's all sorts of couples who'd give their hearts to a little girl called Madison, and you know as well as anyone that fostering—or adoption—can work brilliantly.'

But suddenly once again she heard pain. She could hear it behind the carefully professional words.

She should query it, but there was too much overwhelming her life at the moment to even begin to admit more.

'I don't know how I could have her adopted,' she whispered, and his hands came out and caught her shoulders, holding her steady in the face of her fear. 'But to take her on... A child...'

'You don't need to think of that right now,' he told her. 'You just think of the next half-hour. We need to get a bit of sheep's blood off ourselves so we don't scare the community of Cradle Lake half to death with stories of our bloody exploits. Then we need to go talk to Richard and to Tony and see what Richard has decided to do.'

Richard was sitting up in bed when they arrived back at the house. He was angry. Ginny got that the moment she and Fergus walked around the side of the house. Tony was at his bedside, seated beside him on the veranda. Listening.

Richard was trying to yell. He was gasping for breath but his anger was palpable. Ginny gasped and started forward—but Fergus's hand found her arm and he hauled her back out of sight.

'Let me—'

'Shh.'

'There's no way you can make me,' Richard was saying.

'No one's making you do anything,' Tony responded, his voice unperturbed. 'No one made you do anything five years ago. But it's done, mate. Like the rest of us, you're now facing the consequences.'

'I have no intention—'

'You deny she's your kid?'

'No, but—'

'There you are, then,' Tony said evenly. 'It can happen to us all if we're dumb enough.' He grimaced. 'You know, I got a bit pissed after a footy dinner a few years back. Me and Bridget didn't take precautions. Bang, nine months later, there was Michael, bawling his head off, red-faced and scrawny. My kid. Bridget and I had been pretty keen on each other, so getting married wasn't such a big deal, but we'd intended travelling a bit first, seeing the world before we settled down. Now we have Michael. Lissy followed soon after and here I am, a family man. Whoopee.' Ginny could hear a smile enter his voice. 'You know, now I wouldn't have it any other way.'

'You think I can possibly be interested—'

'Not only interested, but involved, right up to your neck,' Tony said ruthlessly. 'I've seen your kid. Madison. Doc Reynard examined her all over. He says she looks like she hasn't been getting enough to eat. Her mother's obviously been too ill to take proper care of her. And she ran half a mile on gravel to save her mother's life. She lost. That's your kid, Richard. A tough, brave little urchin who looks like you. You want to turn your back on her?'

'Ginny will look after her,' Richard said flatly, and Ginny made to move forward again. Once again Fergus restrained her.

'Not your conversation,' he whispered. 'Shut up and listen.'

'I know where my sister would have told me to go if I'd tried that line on her,' Tony was saying.

'I'm dying.'

'Aren't we all, mate? I could get run over by a bus tomorrow. Hell, that'd leave my Bridget and Michael and Lissy in a right mess.'

'You know what I mean. I'm dying now. How can I be anyone's father?'

'You already are. You just didn't know. This is non-negotiable. What I want to know is if you'll do the right thing if we bring her out here.'

'What the hell do you want me to do?'

'You can't ask this of him,' Ginny whispered, but Fergus's hold was strong and sure and convinced. He had her hand in his, his fingers linked through hers. Reassurance in a crazy world. A notion that she wasn't alone. That he was there for her.

Dumb. It was dumb. She hauled at her hand but it wasn't relinquished.

'You want to see her?' Tony was asking.

'No!'

'Do you mean that?' Tony said softly. He turned. 'Fergus, is that you, mate?'

Their approach had obviously been heard, by Tony at least. Fergus gave Ginny's hand a reassuring squeeze and tugged her round the corner, out where they could be seen.

'Hi,' he said, as if he was dropping in for a casual evening visit. 'Ginny and I have just delivered a lamb. Horribly complicated presentation. Exhausted mother. Only the pure skill of two dedicated doctors could have created the outcome of healthy mum, healthy baby.'

Tony's big face creased into a smile. 'Sheep obstetrics. Multi-talented, huh? Aren't we lucky to have you?'

'Yes,' Fergus said promptly, and Tony laughed. He turned back to Richard. 'You want us to bring out your daughter?'

'I need to speak to Ginny,' Richard said, almost sulkily, but Fergus shook his head, joining the conversation as if he'd heard what had gone before. As indeed he had.

'This isn't Ginny's decision, mate. It's yours.'

'Of course it's Ginny's decision,' Richard said angrily. 'When I die, Ginny will have to—'

'Ginny won't have to do anything. This is your call.'

'I can't get involved in a kid if Ginny won't—'

'Let's leave Ginny out of the equation,' Fergus said, and there was a hint of steel in his voice. 'She has her own life to worry about. She's agreed to do some part-time work with me over the next few weeks.'

Ginny flashed him a look that was pure astonishment but neither man noticed.

'And she won't be around so much. Oh, she'll be around

when you most need her. She's promised you that. But not every waking minute. She'll go under if you ask that of her, and I'm here to treat her as well as you. You made her ill with your suicide bid this afternoon and it's not going to happen again.'

'This is none of your business,' Ginny gasped, but Fergus took her arm again, restraining her from hauling away from his side.

'It's none of Tony's business either, but he's here. You've elected to come to a tiny community and that means people sticking in their oars all over the place. Richard, your daughter's at the hospital and she has no one. If you permit, we'll bring her here and care for her here for as long as you're well enough to cope. If you play it right, when you die she'll retain a memory of a father who cares. Her mother obviously thought that was important. If you don't think it's important then we'll contact the social workers in the city and organise foster-care. You need never see her. Your call, mate. Decide.'

'You can't ask me—' Richard gasped.

'We are asking you.'

'I need to talk to—'

'You don't need to talk to anyone. You make the decision now. You ask to see Madison—your daughter—and we'll bring her to you, with a nurse to help care for her.'

'I don't want a nurse. Ginny can—'

'Ginny can't.' His voice was tough, inflexible, giving no quarter. There was a long silence, broken only by the harsh rasping of Richard's breathing. It wasn't fair, Ginny thought miserably. To ask it of him...

'It's not fair, mate,' Fergus said, in such an unconscious echo of her own thoughts that she gasped. 'But she's your daughter. I have no choice but to put things to you as they are.'

Richard stared up at him. He glanced across at Ginny but Fergus's hand was on her arm protectively, as if he knew that this responsibility would be handed over but there was no way he'd let this happen.

'Tony said she looks like me,' Richard whispered finally, and Fergus nodded.

'She's beautiful. She's battered and she's lost her mother

and she's alone. And, yes, she looks like her father. Do you want to meet her or don't you?'

Ginny held her breath. It could go either way, she thought, and she waited. They all waited.

'I have a daughter?' Richard whispered at last, and something in Fergus's face reacted. It was like a muscle spasm—pain? It was there only momentarily and then gone, but Ginny was sure she'd seen it.

'You have a daughter,' he agreed.

'Then maybe I need to meet her.'

'Only if you agree to a nurse coming to stay as well.'

'There's no need. Ginny will—'

'Ginny won't.'

The two men faced off. Strength facing... Fear?

And strength won. Fergus's determination was implacable and all of them could sense it.

'Fine,' Richard said at last. 'If the kid needs a nurse—'

'If your daughter needs a nurse.'

'My daughter,' Richard said, and the petulance disappeared from his voice. 'My daughter.'

'So we can bring her to her father?

'Yes,' he whispered, and looked up at them. 'Yes, please.'

CHAPTER SIX

WHAT followed were two weeks that Ginny would look back on later as surreal. She didn't know what was happening—only that she had to do what came next.

A search was made for Judith's family. There was a father in New Zealand who hadn't seen her for twenty years and who wanted nothing to do with either burying his daughter or taking responsibility for his grandchild. So Judith was buried in the Cradle Lake cemetery. Richard came in a wheelchair, and, on the advice of a child psychiatrist Fergus had organised to see her, Madison came, too. The little girl seemed impassive, and Ginny held her and watched her and thought of what people had said to her after Chris had died, after Toby had died, after her mother had died. And how nothing had helped.

Fergus stood in the background and said nothing at all. There was this feeling between them, Ginny thought hopelessly as the ceremony moved to its conclusion. It was some sort of intangible link that was somehow just…there. Both of them could feel it, she thought, but neither of them wanted it. It was as if both of them were afraid.

She was afraid, she decided, and she was right to be so. Whatever she felt for Fergus, it had to be sternly set aside.

No involvement.

After the funeral Ginny's back veranda was set up as a hospital ward in miniature. A couple of tradesmen arrived. Refusing payment, they set up a screen that could be pulled back at will. Thus, there could be two rooms. One side was Richard's. The other was Madison's.

The child was stoic. That was the simplest way to describe her, Ginny thought as the days went on. There were no tears. No emotion. Nothing. Tears might have been easier to deal with. What terrors lay behind the expressionless, listless façade?

She voiced her concerns to Fergus and he organised the child psychiatrist from the city to make a second trip to see her. The woman sat by Madison's bed for all of one long afternoon, gently probing, trying to make her talk. At the end the woman wondered whether she should be moved, taken to a specialist unit in Sydney.

That was the first time Richard was moved to anger, surprising them all. 'She stays here,' he snapped. 'This is where she belongs. And push back that damned screen.'

That was a sort of breakthrough. Father and daughter at least seemed aware of each other from then on, although mostly all they did was sleep.

But sometimes Ginny saw Richard watching his daughter with eyes that were sad and yet proud. And when Richard moved, Madison's gaze followed him every inch of the way.

'Don't pressure her,' the child psychiatrist advised before she left. 'She needs time to get used to her new surroundings. To her new…'

She faltered then, because no one could imagine Madison would have time to get used to her new father. Even for the psychiatrist this was new territory.

'It's not fair on Madison,' Ginny told Fergus as the second week ended. Fergus had come out to check on Richard's medication. There was no longer any need for him to treat Madison. The little girl's feet were almost healed. There was no need for her to still be in bed, but whenever they dressed her, whenever they tried to do anything with her, she passively did what they asked, then returned to her bed as soon as she could. 'Maybe we should be doing something more active to cheer her up.'

'The psychiatrist said give her time,' Fergus told her. 'And Richard's her father. He calls the shots.'

Fergus had finished treating Richard at almost the same time as Tony's wife, Bridget, had arrived to take a shift. They'd been walking back to Fergus's truck—a bit self-consciously because that was the way Ginny always was around Fergus. Bridget was 'an occasional nurse when I'm sick of the kids', and her presence was a welcome relief, easing strain. Now she included herself in their conversation, putting in her oar with customary cheerfulness.

'Leave them be,' she advised. 'Talking can sometimes make it worse with kids. I'm the eldest of eight and that was my motto. If you couldn't figure out what to do, then do nothing. This is a funny sort of father-daughter relationship but if that's all they have then I reckon we should leave them to sort it out.'

'Richard's not exactly being warm,' Fergus said thoughtfully as Bridget walked up the steps and left them to it. Ginny wished she hadn't. Fergus was too close for comfort. Whenever he was here he was too close for comfort, she thought. There was this frisson...

'Can you blame him?' she managed. 'If he gets close to his daughter, she'll be hurt all over again when he dies.'

'Yeah,' Fergus said. He looked as if he'd say something else but then thought better of it. Instead, he stepped away from her a little. Maybe he was feeling this frisson as well? 'How are Madison's feet?'

'They're fine. But check them yourself.' She hesitated. They were out of earshot of Richard, Madison or Bridget. The frisson wasn't going away and she wanted it dealt with. She needed this man as a person—not some gorgeous hunk of a doctor who sent her hormones into overdrive.

'Fergus, why are you leaving Madison's medical care completely to me?' she tried tentatively. 'Why don't you go close to her?' She hesitated but the sudden stillness of his face told her she wasn't wrong in her guesswork. 'There's more than Richard and I who are scared stiff of being involved here. No?'

'I don't know what you mean.'

In truth, she didn't know what she meant either. It was just a gut reaction to what she saw—the slight hesitation every time he approached Madison's bed. There was something...

'Hey, Doc, what about taking Ginny out to dinner?' It was Bridget, calling from the veranda. 'She could do with a break and you two look so good together.'

They both took a hasty step in different directions and Bridget grinned.

'I don't need—' Ginny started, but Bridget was on a mission.

'You don't need sausages,' she retorted. 'Which is all you have here for dinner. Richard likes them, Madison likes them but the last time we had them you hardly touched them. Take her out, Doc.'

'Would you like to go out?' Fergus asked.

Would she?

In the last two weeks she hadn't been housebound. She'd spent time at the hospital, sharing Fergus's load, immersing herself in the medicine that gave her blessed time out. But that didn't mean she'd spent any real time with him.

And then there was this scary frisson...

'The pub's good on Friday night,' Bridget was saying, breaking into her train of thought. 'Take her there, Doc.'

'I should stay,' Ginny said, taking another step backward.

'Why?' Bridget demanded, and crossed her arms in disapproval.

'There's no need for you to be here,' she told the nurse, trying to sound decisive. 'You could go home to Tony.'

'I have two kids at home and an untrained puppy. I'm staying here.' Bridget grinned. 'My kids need to bond with their daddy. Tony's done less than his fair share this week and I'm here to stay.'

'Bridget's not going home,' Fergus said. 'That was the agreement when we brought Madison here. There'll be a full-time nurse here all the time.' He hesitated and she saw the same uncertainty in his eyes. But it seemed he was braver than she was. 'What about a steak at the pub?'

But what about...? What about...? Ginny looked at him

and thought about the tension between them and thought this was a really bad idea. But when she opened her mouth...

'Fine,' she said.

What was she saying? Her head was screaming that it wasn't fine. It was high risk to both of them.

'Fine,' said Fergus, and she knew he felt exactly the same way. 'Let's go to dinner.'

The eating-out options at Cradle Lake were limited. To the pub. The pub served steak and chips, sausages and chips (bleah), fish and chips or the vegetarian option catering for city types who cruised through the place on Sundays—pasta and chips.

The steak, however, was fantastic, deservedly famous throughout the district. Dorothy, the pub chef, had been cooking steak for fifty years. She cooked their steaks now, then came to the dining-room door to watch her product go down.

The whole pub watched Fergus and Ginny's steaks go down. The dining room was separated from the rest of the pub by the bar, but from the moment they'd walked in every eye was on them and it stayed on them for the entire meal.

'You wouldn't want to be an undercover agent in this place,' Fergus complained, and Ginny grinned. In truth, she was enjoying her steak very much, and enjoying being away from the claustrophobic atmosphere of the house even more.

'I'm used to it. I was brought up here—remember?'

'Which is why you didn't want to come back?'

'I never said I didn't want to come back.'

'You didn't have to. You look like a deer stuck in headlights.'

'Gee, thanks.'

'Think nothing of it,' he said, and concentrated on his steak again.

'So how about you?' she asked as they ploughed through their massive plates. 'How come you look like a deer caught in headlights as well?'

'I don't.' He glanced up at her, startled, and then caught himself. His expression regained that careful control she was starting to recognise for what it was. A shield.

'I'm the one who's afraid of the commitment Madison might mean,' she said softly. 'But when you're forced to be near her I see exactly the same fear. Only worse. At the funeral you acted as if you were afraid of coming close. So what's happened in your past to drive you here, Dr Reynard?'

'Nothing.'

'You know almost everything there is to know about me,' she went on, suddenly angry. 'Yet you keep yourself hidden. There's a child in there somewhere, isn't there? A tragedy?'

'It's none of your business.'

'Yet my life is your business.'

'That's different. Your brother—'

'Is your patient. Yes. But I'm not your patient. It doesn't stop you poking your nose in. Not that I'm not grateful,' she said hurriedly, as he looked up from his steak. 'You know I am. I've really appreciated the work you've given me over the last couple of weeks—and the freedom. But it's feeling really lopsided. I'm feeling like I'm wandering in a void and part of that is your fault.'

His mouth twisted into a wry smile. 'Gee, thanks.'

'You know what I mean,' she said softly, and met his gaze directly over the table. She'd been trying not to think this for two weeks but it had been there, like it or not, and suddenly it had to be brought out into the open. 'You feel it, too, don't you? This thing…'

'You mean I want to jump you,' he said, and the ears on the other side of the bar almost stretched to where they were sitting. 'Is that the thing you mean?'

'I might not have put it quite like that.' She hesitated and then she smiled, tension easing. 'Do you? Want to jump me?'

'Yes,' he said promptly. 'You want to jump me, too?'

'Fergus…'

'They taught me at medical school to say it like it is,' he said, suddenly cheerful, attacking his steak again with zeal. 'Never prevaricate. If you need to tell bad news then spit it out 'cos otherwise the patient will guess anyway and won't thank you for quibbling.'

'So is this bad news,' she said, after a moment's stunned pause. 'That you want to jump me.'

'Depends on lots of things,' he told her.

'Like?'

'Like I'm not in the market for a permanent relationship.'

'You think I am?'

'I know you're not,' he said, his voice softening so that for the first time she was sure the audience on the other side of the bar couldn't hear. 'Relationships have been beaten out of you the hard way.'

'So how about you?' She placed her knife and fork together over at least half her steak, and at the door Dorothy sighed her disappointment.

Fergus devoured the last mouthful of his steak, hesitated and looked thoughtfully at Ginny's unfinished plate. 'Go right ahead,' she told him, and Dorothy brightened again.

Fergus switched plates in one smooth slide and kept right on eating.

'That doesn't let you off answering the question,' she said. 'If I were to agree to being...jumped...'

'Gee, that's romantic.'

'I'm not sure how else we can put it,' she said. 'A relationship with no involvement.'

'Let's not call it anything.'

'Fine, but I need to know the background,' she retorted. 'You've been married?'

'Yes, but—'

'Who to?'

'Katrina.'

'Where is she now?'

'She's a professor of pathology at a very large hospital in—'

'Katrina Newry,' she interrupted, awed. 'I've heard of her.'

'The world's heard of Katrina.'

'So what went wrong?'

'It's—'

'Only my business if you want to jump me,' she agreed equitably. 'Which you've just agreed you want to do. But I don't go to bed with strangers.'

There was a hushed ripple from the other side of the bar and Ginny thought, Gee the acoustics in here are good. Or terrible, depending on what angle you wanted to look at them from.

'Can this wait until I finish my steak?' Fergus asked, and she knew he'd realised the same thing.

'Fine. Only it's my steak. I'll have coffee while I wait.'

'You don't want pudding?'

'After a steak that hangs over every side of the plate? You have to be kidding.'

'I never kid.'

'I don't want pudding,' she retorted. 'I want history.'

'You—'

'Just shut up and eat,' she told him kindly. 'And then shut up and talk.'

'Pardon?'

'You know what I mean.'

So he finished his steak, they both had coffee and then they walked outside. Fergus had driven them there in his truck-cum-ambulance—it was parked in the car park—but the night was lovely and, of course, the pub had been built to face the lake. There was a track leading down to a spit of land where you could watch the moonlight glimmering on the lake below. Lovers' walk, the locals called it, and Ginny knew every person in the pub would be watching as they turned away from the car park and headed down the track.

It seemed Fergus knew it, too. 'You realise your reputation is shot,' Fergus said morosely. 'Even if we turn and head up to the car park now, they'll assume we were just very, very fast.'

'I'm not fussed about my reputation in this town,' she retorted. 'It's the least of my worries.'

'Because after Richard dies you'll never come here again.'

'That's right.'

'Life was pretty bleak here?'

'What do you think?'

He nodded, then caught her hand as they made their way along the track. It was a simple gesture—boy-girl contact—but it felt good. Dangerously good, Ginny thought. Because she didn't want a relationship and this was teetering remarkably close to feeling...

Close.

Dumb. She didn't do close. Neither did he, apparently.

She needed to find out his reasons. Maybe they could reinforce hers.

'You turn away from Madison like you're in pain,' she said softly into the stillness of the night, and she felt the sudden tension in the link between their fingers. 'Why?'

'I don't—'

'I'm right. There was a child, wasn't there?'

'I—'

'Tell me about her.' They'd reached the spit now. There was a seat—a vast gum tree that had fallen sixty years before. The locals had sheared off the rough bark so it lay now as a huge bench seat almost twenty feet long.

They were the only lov— The only people here tonight. Below lay the lake, and around them lay the entire valley, swathed in moonlight. Up above, there were still people in the pub but the acoustics of the valley meant that sound rose, didn't fall. They were swathed in silence and in moonlight.

There was nothing to stop secrets being told here. Except reluctance.

Fergus pulled his hand away but it was Ginny who held on as they sat, sensing that if she was gaining strength from this contact then so would he.

'A daughter?' she asked softly, guessing, and he nodded.

'Molly.'

'Is she with her mother?'

'She's dead.' It was said with flat vehemence, almost shocking in the beauty of the night.

'Oh, Fergus...'

'You're sorry? Everyone's sorry.' He pulled his hand from hers, and raked long fingers through his hair in a gesture of weariness. 'That was uncalled for,' he told her. 'I apologise. Of course you're sorry and it's not that I mind, but…'

'I do know,' she whispered. 'When Toby died, and then Chris, and then my mum… I thought if anyone else said sorry… When did she die?'

'Three months ago.'

'So recently?' She flinched. 'Why? How?'

'Molly had Down's syndrome. She had a congenital heart defect. We knew from birth that she had a limited time.'

She didn't say anything. She couldn't.

'You didn't need to be loaded with that,' he said at last, and she flinched.

'I walk around in my own little ball of misery and don't see others. I should see. I'm sorry I didn't sense this before.'

'You cope with what you need to cope with,' he said gently. 'It's called triage. You only have so much capacity and that has to be channelled where it's most needed. There's no point being sad for me.' He smiled then and rose, looking down at her with almost a challenge. 'And it's not all sad,' he said. 'Molly had a great life, even if it was short.'

'And…your wife?'

His face stilled. Hardened. 'Remember I told you it is possible to be detached? Katrina took one look at her baby and detached. She didn't want to be a part of Molly's life. She walked away. Cut ties. More fool her. If she knew what she missed out on…'

'But it's still awful,' Ginny said hesitantly. 'When you look at Madison…'

'Then I see Molly,' he agreed. 'Or I see what Molly might have been, if there'd been just one more chromosome.'

'And you're in Cradle Lake because?'

'The hospital where I worked… Molly attended day care there. We lived in a hospital apartment, and when I worked at weekends Molly was there with me. The nursing staff—everyone—loved her almost as much as I did. When Molly died, it was like the whole hospital went into mourning. In the end I needed to get away from everyone else's grief as well as my own.'

'So you've been flung straight into my tragedy.'

'I'm not in anyone's tragedy,' he said roughly. 'I'm on the outside, looking in. Which is how I'm facing the world from here on. Which is how I suggest you face it.'

'But Madison...'

'Ginny, there are wonderful potential parents out there who are aching to have a little girl like Madison. You know as well as I do how hard it is to find a child to adopt. You also know that you, as her guardian when Richard dies, will have a say in choosing those parents and you'll have rights to access as she grows up. When Richard dies, you can step away. You know you can. You can live your own life.'

'I don't think—'

'You can,' he said, softly but strongly. He reached forward suddenly and seized her hands, tugging her to her feet. Standing so she was right before him and he was looking down at her in the moonlight. 'You're a woman of strength, Ginny Viental, and you can use your strength to keep yourself independent.'

'Right. So standing here now, with you holding my hands, looking at me like this, that'd be independent.'

'I can be independent and still want to kiss you.'

'Yeah?'

'Sure,' he said, and if there was a trace of defiance in his tone, both of them ignored it.

Because...maybe both of them knew it was impossible. Or at the least risky.

But there was suddenly no way that kiss wasn't going to happen.

He was so big, Ginny thought. So male. So...gentle? Gentle was the wrong word, but it was all she had. He stood looking down at her, smiling quizzically in the moonlight, and it was as if for the first time in her life someone knew her. Someone could see what was underneath the carefully cultivated layers.

But she didn't feel exposed, because what lay under those layers, the fears and the void of loss, were the same for both of them. This man shared something she'd thought was hers alone.

Trust. The word entered her subconscious and stayed there.

She could trust him because he knew her. And that trust…

Its sweetness was almost a siren song. She gazed up into his face and he looked back and his eyes were gently asking if he could take the next step…

The next step in trust?

To kiss.

She smiled back at him, albeit a shaky smile, a smile full of uncertainty but a smile for all that.

He kissed her.

And her world changed, just like that.

Ginny had dated before. Of course she had. She was almost thirty and she was no innocent. She'd carefully held herself at arm's length when it came to letting her heart get involved but she enjoyed a great social life.

But she'd never felt…

What?

She didn't know. It was some indefinable factor, but it slammed into her with such force that it shook her to the core. The moment Fergus's mouth met hers, it was different in a way she could never have imagined. Could never have dreamt of.

Her heart stopped beating.

What a dumb thought. Of course it didn't stop. She was a sensible person. She was a doctor. This was the stuff of romance novels. A kiss changing things…

She made to pull back and he released her, his eyes searching her face in the moonlight.

'You don't want this?'

'I… Yes, I do,' she whispered. 'Or I think I do. But I don't do relationships.' Her voice was almost fearful.

'Of course you don't. Wise girl. Neither do I. But kissing…'

'You know as well as I do that this isn't going to stop at kissing.'

He stilled. There was a moment's pause—a regroup. This was the time for them both to pull away. But his hands were holding hers and the feel of his mouth was still on her lips. The taste of him. How could she pull away?

'You're a really desirable woman,' he said, and there was a trace of uncertainty in his voice now. 'I'd be lying if I said I didn't want you.'

'But you don't do relationships.'

'No.' Still there was that uncertainty and it scared her.

'You promise,' she said, and her voice was urgent.

The smile came back into his voice then—and into his eyes. They crinkled at the edges, the laughter lurking behind. A big, gentle man who took on the troubles of the world...

'You're saying we can make love as long as I agree to take off like a cad at first light.'

'There's a lot to be said for cads,' she whispered, and managed to smile back.

'No strings,' he murmured.

'N-no strings.'

'You're sure?'

She looked at his face in the moonlight and she felt fear. A sensible woman would retreat right now, she thought. But...

But she'd suddenly had it with being a sensible woman. Life was suddenly far too bleak. The future was suddenly far too scary. Heaven knew what would happen tomorrow—she certainly didn't.

They'd both seen too much grey, she thought, and if she was suddenly defiant rather than sensible, who could blame her? The night was still and warm. This man was right before her. Back at home lay...

No. Don't think of that. She could see from Fergus's eyes that he was feeling exactly what she was. He needed this night and so did she.

And she'd take it. No matter how stupid. No matter how dumb.

'I don't suppose,' she whispered, 'that you have a condom at hand?'

There was a moment's hush. The laughter faded and then sprang back again.

'Can you doubt it? I'm a doctor. Up in my truck I have a doctor's bag with almost a fully equipped pharmacy inside it. Ginny, are you sure?'

'That means we have to go via your truck, right?'

'Um…yeah.' His hands pulled her into him, holding her close. 'There's probably all sorts of creepy-crawlies here anyway. Snakes and stuff.'

'Probably,' she agreed equitably. 'And snakes—and stuff— are decidedly unsexy. I know a better place.'

'There you are then,' He grinned. 'I have a condom, you have a place—what more do we want?'

'Each other,' she whispered. 'For tonight. But just for tonight, Fergus.'

'Just for tonight,' he agreed. 'No strings. But, Ginny…'

'Mmm?'

'For tonight I'm going to love you.'

CHAPTER SEVEN

GINNY had no intention of returning to the house. Neither did she want to go Fergus's apartment, attached via a connecting door to the hospital, with all the connotations that held.

But down on the lake was the Viental boatshed. In her awful teenage years, Ginny had used it as a refuge. She'd gone there when life had simply overwhelmed her. It didn't seem like home. It didn't seem like any other place. It was simply the boatshed—her retreat from the world.

She directed Fergus. They drove in silence, with Fergus every now and then glancing across at her, as if reassuring himself that she was still there. Still real.

She sat with her hands clasped loosely on her knees and tried not to think the same of him. This was a moment out of time, she thought. One grasped moment of unreality, a gift not to be extended. A magic disappearing gift, here for tonight but gone in the morning. The contact with someone who shared... her heart?

Let's not be fanciful, she told herself, but her lips curved in a tiny smile that wasn't quite mockery. She looked sideways and found Fergus was smiling as well. An echo?

Just for tonight, she told herself. Just for tonight.

The world was holding its breath.

The boatshed was nestled in a patch of natural bushland just off the road. Fergus pulled the car onto the verge. He grabbed his jacket from over the seat and Ginny grinned.

'You need a jacket?'

'My phone's in the pocket,' he said apologetically, and her smile died.

'Medical imperatives, huh?'

'I did agree to take this job.'

'Are we expecting medical imperatives?'

'They'd have to be pretty damned imperative. You unlock the boatshed. I'll get my bag out of the back.'

'Because it contains medical imperatives?'

'Absolutely.'

Was this wrong? Ginny hauled open the boatshed door, feeling like she should be feeling qualms. Or conscience. Or worry. Or something. She felt none of those things. She just felt…right.

By the time Fergus followed she had the doors open on the other side of the shed. This was a dry shed, with the boat having to be winched up a tracked ramp to be under cover. The boat the family had used had long been sold, but the shed itself was weatherproof and completely dry.

Ginny had always loved it. It had become a bolthole, when things had been too awful at home, and she'd squirrelled things away here. Blankets. Pillows. An old mattress, with a couple of broken springs. Her comforts were ancient but not so old they couldn't be very useful now.

Fergus stopped at the door and gazed around in appreciation. The moon was almost full, and as soon as Ginny flung open the boat doors onto the lake, the moonlight flooded in.

'I have candles,' Ginny said, a trifle self-consciously and he nodded.

'I bet you have. With little cupids engraved…'

'There's no need to mock.'

'I'm not mocking,' he said softly, grinning. 'Ginny, this is magic. A man could fall in love…'

'But you won't.'

'Of course I won't,' he said, though he suddenly sounded a trace unsure. He came up behind her and placed his hands on her shoulders, turning her to face him. His smile faded. 'Ginny, are you sure?'

'About tonight? I'm as sure as I've ever been about anything. But tomorrow…there's no tomorrow, Fergus. We both know that.'

'So we do,' he said gently. 'But there is tonight.'

She looked up at him, fixing her eyes on his. Making sure. And then, suddenly, before any more of these stupid scruples could get in the way, she tugged her shirt over her head. Then she flicked the fasteners of her bra, letting it fall free, and reached for the zip of her jeans.

He caught her hand.

'This is not an offering you're making,' he said softly, catching her other hand as well and holding her before him. 'This is mutual love-making we're indulging in here. Mutual. I want you, Ginny, but I want you to want me.'

'I do want you,' she whispered.

'Not for sex, Ginny. For love-making. Whether or not there's a tomorrow, this needs to be an act of love or I want no part of it. I need you to kiss me.'

She gazed up at him. He was looking down at her, but he wasn't looking at her breasts, as some men might have. He was searching her eyes.

He was so…so….

There was something changing inside her. Something she hadn't been aware could be changed.

Fergus.

She twisted the grip of his hand so it was she who was doing the holding. She lifted his hand high, so the back of his hand was against her cheek. So she could feel the roughness of his skin against her.

This was so right. For this night, this was her man. He was big and tender and scarred with the same horror she'd faced. She put her hands up and touched his face, gently, tenderly, never letting her eyes move from his.

'Fergus.'

He bent and he kissed her.

And in that instant her world readjusted itself. The awful tilted axis somehow righted itself. Love-making, he'd called it, and maybe it was the right description. For now, for this wondrous moment, the horror of commitment made way for…

For what? She wasn't asking and neither was he. Because wonderfully, inevitably, Fergus was merging his mouth with hers. Her hands were cradling his face, brushing his cheek with her fingers, tracing the roughness of skin, and for this moment she was loving every inch of him.

He deepened the kiss, and the sensation made her want to cry out in pleasure. But she couldn't, for to do that would be to break the moment. To take pause…

But he did take pause. He moved back then, just a little, so she could see the flare of desire in his eyes but could also read the sudden doubt.

'Ginny, it is love-making.'

'Yes, but only for tonight. Just for tonight,' she whispered, knowing it was what he wanted to hear but suddenly no longer sure that her words held truth. She smiled up at him, forcing her smile to be that of a calm, sure woman, with the situation totally in her control. The fact that the situation was suddenly totally out of control was no fault of his and it was no less magical for that. For the first time in her life she was out of control, and glorying in it.

Please…

The word was no sooner formed in her mind before she had her answer. She was being kissed again, and it seemed she'd been waiting all her life for this kiss.

Her lips parted, joy surging through her body as she realised that hesitations were gone. For this moment things had indeed changed. He was her Fergus—the man who'd lain beside her and rescued a lamb and somehow changed the way she viewed her world.

She closed her eyes, aching with sensual pleasure as he deepened the kiss. His fingers were holding her, tracing the contours of her waist, seeking to know her. He was glorying in the smoothness of her skin, slowly, wonderingly, and each inch of movement sent shivers of sheer sensual pleasure through her entire body.

She let herself lean into him, letting her body's weight be supported by his, seeking reassurance that he was real and not some romantic fantasy. Not some dream that would dissipate before it went further. That this was happening in truth and not in dreams. She was naked to the waist and he was still clothed, but that was of no concern. She could feel the strength of him underneath. The clothes would disappear in time and for now it seemed they had all the time in the world.

'For tonight I love you, Fergus,' she whispered. 'This is indeed love-making.'

'It is indeed.' He held her at arm's length. 'Ginny, are you indeed sure? You know I make no promises.'

'I want no promises. For now I just want you.'

He gazed down into her eyes for a long, long moment, questioning, probing, but her answers had already been given.

'My beloved fool. We're both fools.'

'No. We're a mature man and woman with a condom. Out to have a very good time.' She smiled up at him, aware that her whole universe was centred in this one moment, and she caught his hand and held. She kissed every finger in turn while he gazed down at her bent head with wonder in his eyes.

He kissed her once more but it was different. Better. He kissed her as she needed to be kissed. As she ached to be kissed. Her neck, her lips, her eyelids.

She lifted his hand and led it to her breast. He slipped his fingers around the soft swell, cupping the smooth contours, tracing the nipples, making her cry out in a soft, low ache of need and desire and love.

He was still in his shirt and she needed him closer. She needed the fabric to be gone. The night was dreamlike and wonderful as she pulled away. The flickering rays of moonlight off the water were playing on their faces. There was no need of candlelight here.

Her Fergus. For tonight, this was her Fergus.

They didn't speak. There was no room for speaking. There

was no need. Her fingers were unfastening the front of his shirt. He watched her, his hands gently touching her face, and she could hear his breathing deepening as she made her way downward. Her fingers were feeling the warmth of his skin under the fabric. Her lovely Fergus. Her hero, wounded as she was, but for this night magically healed.

His breathing was becoming ragged as she ran her hands over his chest, feeling his hair between her fingers. Leaning closer, she kissed his neck, tasting the salt of him. Loving him. The shirt had fallen away and he was left with only his jeans.

Her Fergus. Hers.

She locked his arms behind him, then lifted her head to allow him to kiss her. He was tasting her neck, caressing her shoulders with his tongue and the sensation was so exquisite she thought she must cry out in pleasure. She could hardly breathe. She stood motionless, gasping her pleasure as he lowered his head and kissed between her breasts. Slowly. Slowly. His hands gently cupped each breast and his lips moved from one to the other. He kissed them in turn, tantalising, teasing the proudly upright nipples. Savouring.

His fingers moved, gently, whispering down her back, her arms, neck… And then he tugged her into him and their heated bodies moulded together.

Skin to skin.

Their mouths were joined again, her hands holding him in urgent, primeval need. His hands tugged at her hips and she felt her jeans slipping. Good. This was right. She searched for the zipper of his and tugged, and her hands kept on tugging. Away. Away. As his clothing disappeared, her hands stayed at his hips. She felt his body stiffen with shock as her fingers found what they were seeking.

And she found what for this moment she desired above all else. That which would link her to this man in a way she must be if she was to live.

She was under no illusion now. This night was changing her, hauling her out of a dark abyss that she could no longer bear to be in. The escape for her was in loving this man, whether he wanted her or not. But joyously he did want her. For this moment, and that was all that mattered. It was all that could be allowed to matter.

Their bodies were melting into each other. He tugged her closer, then swept her up into his arms and lowered her onto the ancient mattress. She heard herself cry out with dismay as they were momentarily separated, as he did what he needed to do to keep them safe. But it was done in an instant and then he joined her, his body melting against hers.

Slow. Tender. Inevitable. Their bodies curved against each other, and as they met, skin against skin, she felt herself growing dizzy with passion she'd never known. That she'd never realised she could know.

Oh, the feel of him. The joy. He kissed her neck, a rain of kisses, running his tongue over her smooth, soft skin, while his magic hands caressed the hot skin of her breasts, her navel, her belly and beyond.

He was so beautiful. This magnificent body, strong and virile, in full manhood. What right did he have to turn away from loving because he'd once been hurt?

Fergus.

They lay entwined on the mattress and the night air warmed their naked skin, creating an intimacy far greater than any closed bedroom door. The night was warm and still, and the tiny waves from the lake were slapping against the boatshed floor. There were plovers calling along the grassland on the shore, their calls eerie and wonderful. Every sense was aroused—she was aware of every nuance—she'd never felt so alive as she did at this moment.

'Fergus,' she whispered, her voice husky with passion, and he rolled on top of her in one lithe move. He was above her then, his knees holding her hips within the strong bounds of his thighs. She arched upward, aching to be closer, closer, kissing his chest, breathing hard, tasting the salt of him.

Fergus.

She was moaning now, kissing him, clutching his back, aching for him to be inside her, but he held himself still. His arms were hard and sinewy as he held himself up, drawing out the moment she so longed for.

She arched again, but he leaned forward and kissed her deeply, his tongue caressing, promising, giving a foretaste of what was to come.

'My beautiful girl,' he whispered. 'My crazy fool. My heart.'

'Come into me.' Her thighs were aching with need, her body was creating a flame all of its own, but still he resisted. He lowered himself, but not where she most needed him. Instead, he laid his chest lightly against her breasts, brushing, over and back, over and back, until her breasts felt as if they were alive and her whole body was trembling with want and ache and love.

Still he brushed, over and over, and then he kissed her, every part of her, moving languorously from her lips to her neck, to her breasts, down over her belly, taunting the aching need within until she thought she could die right at this minute and know that here was paradise.

Enough. Enough. She took his body and held in a fierce possessive hug that had him centred exactly where he needed to be centred, lowering exactly where he needed to lower— and he was there.

She buried her face in his shoulder and she knew she was weeping. He was deep inside her, strong and gentle, plundering yet loving. She moved with him, her body taking her rhythm from his, letting him take her where he wanted but assuaging her own need, reaching her heart, taking her to where she was meant to be.

Taking her to a home she'd never known she could have.

Her eyes were wide in the moonlight as he loved her and loved her still. How could she close her eyes on this wonder? His body in the night was a thing of raw strength and beauty. She marvelled at his beauty as he moved above her, as he loved her. His body was glistening with sweat, with concentration, with desire.

Her man. For tonight, her man. Her path to the future.

But then she stopped thinking. Thoughts gave way to pure

sensation as her body reacted to the moment, to his strength, to his love, to her aching, tearing need. The night and the moonlight and the sounds of the waters of the lake merged into her feeling for this man, this wondrous fulfilment of passion that had her crying out, arching, her body moving without her willing it, taking its need and causing the night to merge into a mist of heat and stars and white-hot love.

It went on and on, surging throughout her body, and the moment the sensation eased, another started to build, in a long rolling, burning heat. Over and over. She wept and her hands clutched his body and she knew that her world was right here.

Her love.

And when it finished, when finally he lay back exhausted, still he held her. His arms cradled her and she moulded herself to his body and she felt his heartbeat and knew that in her world things were finally right.

She found the strength to raise herself over him and she kissed him, on the eyelids, on his cheeks, on his mouth, gently, tenderly. He gazed up at her with eyes that were spent from passion but still held all the tenderness she could desire.

'Oh, God, Ginny…'

'God has nothing to do with it,' she whispered, allowing a touch of severity to enter her voice. 'And if he has, I hope he has his eyes closed. For an unmarried woman to take such pleasure…'

'No god could deny you pleasure,' he whispered. 'After the things you've faced…have yet to face…'

'You mean, if I sleep now I'll wake up and see you naked in the dawn?' she demanded, refusing to be drawn where he was taking her, and he chuckled, a deep, glorious chuckle that had her heart twist in a way it had never twisted in its existence.

'Scared?'

'I guess I'm not,' she said, smiling and burying her face in his chest. 'You are the most extraordinarily sexy man.'

'I know,' he said modestly, and she giggled.

'Ginny…'

'Hush,' she whispered, suddenly realising what he might

say and knowing she didn't want to go there. 'OK, Fergus, you're extraordinary. But are you going to prove it or are you going to sleep? If you're extraordinary…'

'What?'

'Then you'd be making love to me again. Right now. Your call, Fergus.'

And it was no call at all. He gazed at her for a long time and laughter died and she saw the doubts were still there behind the laughter.

'My Ginny,' he whispered. 'My dream, my heart, my love. My beautiful, golden girl. How can you need me? It can't be real. It can't last. But for now… You're here, you're my woman, and you want me. You're a miracle that's here for the taking and I can't refuse you, my love.'

'And why would you want to?' she demanded with some asperity, and the corners of his mouth twitched into a crooked smile.

'Why indeed?'

He tugged her down to him, his mouth claimed hers and the whole glorious cycle started again.

Until the phone rang.

Until the medical imperative took over.

She didn't go with him. There were yet two hours before dawn and this sounded like a simple case of a child with gastroenteritis. One doctor could handle this alone so Fergus could go play doctor and she could stay here and play abandoned lover in the moonlight.

Which suited her mood entirely. But she didn't feel in the least abandoned.

She lay in what was left of the moonlight, staring out at the shimmering surface of the lake.

She'd sworn never to come back here. This place had been her refuge as a child but as an adult it had represented a security she knew was an illusion.

Was it an illusion? Happy ever after?

'It'll end,' she whispered into the night. 'It'll end in tears.

'But maybe not yet. Maybe I could give this loving business one more chance.

'You'll be hurt.

'Yes, but if I don't try…'

She rolled over and the mound of blankets where Fergus had lain was still warm. She buried her face in his pillow and thought she could smell him.

'Now I am being a lovesick teenager. He doesn't want me.

'Even if he doesn't…'

He was off saving the world, she thought. Off being busy, trying to block out pain, trying not to let love creep in at the edges.

He had so much love to give.

'So do I,' she told the lake. 'I thought I didn't. But tonight…it's crazy but suddenly there's more room. For Fergus…'

For whoever.

Fergus might or might not want her for much longer, she thought, and she could cope with that. She had no choice. Tonight had been magic—a wonderful time out for both of them and for her an experience that had resettled her world on an axis it had been shaken off so many years before.

But for Fergus… His pain was raw and new and he'd had no time to adjust to the awfulness of loss. To expect tonight to change him…

'It won't,' she told the darkened lake, and she saw the light fade as the moon slipped beneath the horizon to the west. Soon it would be dawn.

Could she cope with it?

'I surely can,' she said, and sat up and hugged her knees. Then she put out a hand and laid it on the ancient floorboards. 'Touch wood.

'It'll take guts.

'Yeah, but it feels so good…connecting…' She hugged her knees some more as if she was reassuring a friend. As if she could conjure up Fergus's body in her arms.

'It'll hurt again.

'I know. But it hurts anyway, and I'm so tired of feeling

empty. Dammit, I'm going to try.' She stared around the ancient boatshed and realised what had happened.

'I swore never to come back here,' she told herself. 'And here I am—back.'

Fergus drove toward the Horace farm feeling…odd. Like he'd just been hauled back from a precipice and he wasn't at all sure he appreciated the sensation.

He'd been so close to toppling over.

Once when he'd been a young intern in a busy emergency room, an ancient lady had suffered a cardiac arrest on his shift. He'd done what he'd been trained to do. He'd called for the crash cart, he'd applied the defibrillator, he'd worked on her hard for fifteen minutes—and he'd got her back. It had felt great.

But two days later he'd visited her in the ward and when she'd realised who he was she'd hurled her bowl of hospital broth at him with more force than such a woman could reasonably have been expected to possess.

'I was ready,' she'd hissed. 'They've all gone before me. My husband. My friends. Two of my children. They were waiting and I was ready and you hauled me back. For what? What, young man? What?'

It had been a salutary lesson, and now he made a huge effort to learn which of his patients would elect to give the order 'not for resuscitation.'

Which should have no bearing on how he was feeling now, he thought dryly, but it did. He'd lain with Ginny in his arms and he'd felt so close to declaring himself in love. He'd gone so close to tumbling into the whole relationship thing again and now that he'd been pulled back…

Now that he'd been pulled back he was feeling sick and empty. Maybe…just maybe loving again wouldn't be so bad.

Just Ginny, he told himself hastily in case his mind should get any funny ideas about taking it further. Maybe Ginny and I could have some sort of relationship. The thought of holding her again, of lying with her, of burying his body in hers, was infinitely appealing. And Ginny didn't want attachments. She wouldn't want children. They could be a career couple, carefully independent but meeting somewhere…

Meeting where? In marriage?

His mind closed on the idea—but then the thought of Ginny rose up before him. He let the image stay and the more he let it drift in his mind the more seductive the image grew.

'Just Ginny,' he said into the darkness. 'If she'll have me. If she'll let some of her precious independence go. Not that I want her to be dependent…'

What did he want?

And the answer came back.

He wanted Ginny.

His cellphone rang again and he clicked through to the speaker on his truck console.

'You on your way, Doc?' It was Clive Horace, sounding anxious. 'Stephanie's just chucked again and that makes it five times since midnight. Won't she be getting dehydrated?'

Yeah, Fergus thought, shoving away the image of the seductive Ginny until he had more time to focus. Stephanie would. He needed to concentrate on medicine.

Ginny would have to wait.

But not very long, he told himself fiercely. She was still at the boatshed, lying sleepily in her cocoon of ancient blankets.

Maybe if he was fast…

He wouldn't be fast. If Stephanie had vomited five times since midnight, she'd probably need to be admitted.

Medicine was for now.

Ginny was for tomorrow.

Their paths didn't cross in the morning. Ginny came into the hospital early and spent two hours running a prenatal clinic she'd organised. She'd done it simply by putting a notice in the window of the general store.

"If you're pregnant and would like your check-ups done here instead of Bowra, come along on Tuesday morning."

The obstetrician in Bowra was delighted to have pressure taken off what was a vast workload, and Ginny ended up with twelve ladies to see. She did the antenatal checks but it ended up as an impromptu get-together of Cradle Lake's prospective mums—something just as valuable as any medical advice she could have given.

Fergus came in at the end, but Ginny had just left.

'She's left us to natter,' one of the ladies—a woman who by the look of her was planning on delivering her entire family in one hit—told him. 'Oh, but she's lovely. We were just telling her that when you leave we'll try to persuade her to stay, and she didn't say no. Wouldn't that be fantastic?'

Fantastic?

Fergus frowned. Richard didn't have long left. Ginny would leave straight away—he was certain of that. She'd organise Madison's adoption and then head back to the city.

Which was where their relationship could maybe become something they could take seriously. Maybe they could take a step or two toward permanence.

Hell, it had been a one-night stand so far, he told himself, startling himself with where his thoughts were going. He'd made love to a woman who'd made him feel alive again, and it had started him thinking that maybe he didn't need to cut himself right off from the world.

Fine. But one step at a time. If it worked out...

It had to work out.

No, it didn't, he told himself, saying farewell to the happy cluster of mums-to-be and striding out to the truck to take a quick ride out to see Richard. He'd promised to drop in on Richard this morning and it was almost lunchtime.

And Ginny would be there.

There was no reason at all for his steps to quicken as he strode out of the hospital toward...

Toward Ginny?

His steps definitely quickened.

CHAPTER EIGHT

THERE were dogs at Ginny's farmhouse.

Fergus pulled into the yard and he could see things had changed. There was a fenced-off area to one side of the veranda, a temporary construction of chicken wire and garden stakes.

There were three dogs inside the pen and Ginny was sitting in the middle of them.

Up on the veranda sat Madison. Every time he'd come she'd been sitting lethargic and uninterested. Now she was sitting on the top step, watching with what seemed almost eagerness.

Richard was still in bed. He was getting weaker by the day and it was too much to expect him to get up now, but Tony had hauled his bed around so that he, too, could watch. Tony was sitting on the end of the bed, overseeing the entire proceedings.

This was some strange hospital.

'You're going to have to be polite if you want some hot dog,' Ginny was saying, and he hauled his attention back to her without any effort at all. 'Sit.'

What was she doing?

Three dogs. Three disreputable mutts. One looked like some sort of whippet, long, rangy and lean. There was a black and white border collie with a little bit of kelpie thrown in for good measure, and there was a little dog, a wiry-looking terrier who looked sharply intelligent. It was this dog Ginny was addressing. The other two were already seated, waiting expectantly.

While he watched, the little dog gave a tentative yap.

'Your friends are waiting,' Ginny said. 'You sit and you all get a bit of hot dog. Sit, sir.'

'Yap.'

'You heard what I said.'

The dog stood four square and looked at Ginny. Ginny sat on the grass and eyeballed the dog straight back.

'You want the hot dog? Then sit.' She raised the hot dog over the little dog's head so it was forced to look up. She pressed the dog's chest very gently.

The dog sat.

'Well done,' she said, and beamed, and handed out three pieces of hot dog.

From the veranda came the sound of clapping. Fierce clapping from Tony. Faint clapping from Richard. And— amazingly—an even fainter clapping from Madison.

'What's going on?' he demanded, and all eyes swivelled to Fergus. The dogs reacted with startled aggression, hurling themselves against the chicken wire.

'Hey,' Ginny said. 'Manners. You want more hot dog? Quiet!'

Her last word was a roar. Three tails went between six back legs. 'Sit,' she said, and beamed as they sat. She promptly distributed more hot dog.

'They're Oscar's dogs,' he said on a note of discovery, and she grinned and climbed over the chicken wire.

'I knew you were clever.'

'Why are Oscar's dogs here?'

'Ginny always was fabulous with dogs,' Richard managed, giving his sister a faint smile.

She bounded up the veranda steps, three at a time, reached the bed and gave her brother a hug.

'I still am. I still will be. Weren't they great?'

'My daddy likes dogs,' Madison said cautiously, and Richard smiled at his daughter.

'Your daddy certainly does.' He had to stop there—energy

was fading as they watched—but some sort of link had definitely been made, Fergus thought. *My daddy*... Things had happened since he'd been here last.

'Oscar had six dogs,' he said, feeling his way.

Ginny plumped down on the step beside Madison and hauled her in so they were linked hard, side by side.

'These are the good dogs. The others had to go to a home for bad dogs.'

Fergus stared at the dogs. He stared at Richard and then at Ginny and Madison. Then he turned to the nurse on duty. 'Do you know what's going on?'

'You know Oscar's agreed to stay in the nursing home?' Tony asked, and Fergus nodded.

'Yeah.'

'The council ranger called at the place yesterday,' Tony told him. 'Ginny's been feeding the dogs and caring for the stock in general. One of the neighbouring farmers has agreed to take on the sheep until things are sorted out but no one wants the dogs. Oscar's said he doesn't care, so the ranger told Ginny yesterday that he'd take them to...' He hesitated and glanced at Madison. 'To the dogs' home.'

'Right,' Fergus said, still feeling his way. He looked at the way Ginny was hugging Madison and he thought, She's changed. Something's definitely changed.

Was it the way he thought about Ginny?

Sure, that had changed, but there was more. Until yesterday Ginny had treated Madison with kindness. She'd held her at the funeral. She'd treated her feet, she'd told her stories, she'd done the physical caring, but there'd been that tiny distancing. A professional distancing, he'd thought.

Today there was no such distance. Today she was hugging Madison as if she meant it.

'I went over this morning,' Ginny told him, still hugging Madison. 'On the way back from...where I'd been. I knew the whippet—or sort of. Years ago, when we left our farm, Oscar took over our two dogs. He always liked a dog pack, even if he never trained them, and back then when I was a teenager it was either leave our dogs with Oscar or have them put down. The social worker who…who took me away said I didn't have a choice.' She gestured down to the whippet in the pen. 'I'm guessing this one's related. Anyway, I ran them all through their paces.'

'Paces?'

He still sounded cautious, he thought, but it behoved him to be cautious. He'd come out here with plans for himself which just might include Ginny. But suddenly Ginny's side of the equation didn't look quite as uncomplicated as it had last night.

'I fed them and took their food away halfway through their meal,' she said. 'I'd fed them last night so they weren't all that hungry but, despite that, three of them tried to bite me. The other three looked at me like I was being mean but they let me do it. That was test one. I sat down with them for an hour and at the end of the hour I had the three non-biters on my knee, all telling me they were prepared to be devoted. The other three took themselves off to the other side of the yard and refused to be friendly.'

'She'd gone over prepared to take on the whippet,' Richard whispered into the silence. 'Trust our Ginny to bring back three. Her heart's bigger than the *Titanic*. Only it's different. It's unsinkable.'

He subsided. Fergus glanced at him, concerned, and gestured Tony to adjust the oxygen flow. Tony gave an almost imperceptible shrug, which told him a hundred per cent oxygen was already running.

Richard's time was fast running out. Maybe a week, Fergus thought. Maybe less. He looked back at Ginny and saw the wash of pain cross her face. He knew that his diagnosis had found concurrence.

'Is there anything you need?' he asked softly, but he was asking the question more of Tony than of Richard. Richard had slumped into sleep. Soon his sleep would be more than that.

'Things are fine,' Ginny whispered, tugging Madison up onto her knee and burying her face in her hair. 'Your daddy's sick but he's not hurting, is he, love? He's gone to sleep now. Soon he'll sleep all the time.'

'My daddy and mummy are going to be together,' Madison whispered, so softly that Fergus had to stoop to hear her. 'But Ginny and the puppies will look after me.'

What…? Fergus stared down at Ginny as if she'd taken leave of her senses. 'What are you saying?' he asked, and she gave him a rueful smile.

'What I ought to have been saying two weeks ago. The heart expands to fit all comers.'

'Sorry?'

'I went to Oscar's to get a dog,' she said. 'One dog. Only two other dogs put their heads on my knee and I thought, OK, I can fit three dogs into my life.'

'In your hospital apartment?'

'Things might have to change.'

'How?'

'I think I might make a cup of tea,' Tony announced into an atmosphere that was suddenly charged. 'Does anyone else want a cup of tea?'

'I'd love one,' Ginny told him, and gave him a grateful smile.

'You want to come with me?' Tony asked Madison. 'There's cookies with smiley faces in the biscuit barrel.'

'You've been making cookies?' Fergus was so astounded that he almost barked the question, and Madison flinched at the unexpected noise. He winced. 'Sorry,' he told the little girl. 'I didn't know your… I didn't know Ginny knew how to make cookies.'

'I don't,' Ginny agreed. 'One of the neighbours brought over a bunch of baking. But I might learn.'

'You might learn.' He stood, feeling winded, while Tony gathered Madison up and carried her into the house. Richard had seemingly drifted into a deep, untroubled sleep. There was suddenly only Fergus and Ginny.

And the future?

Ginny was silent. Fergus hesitated, then sat on the step beside Ginny and stared out over the yard. The dogs had slumped into a pile of canine contentment in the shade of a cotoneaster. Ginny looked as if she was watching them.

Maybe she was, but who knew what she was seeing?

They remained silent for a couple of minutes. Ginny didn't seem inclined to talk and Fergus was struggling to find the right words. He didn't know the right words.

'Ginny…' he said softly at last, and she nodded.

'Mmm?'

'Last night was fantastic.'

'It was, wasn't it?' she agreed, and there was a note of smugness in her voice that had him taken aback.

'You agree?'

'Mind-blowing sex,' she said in satisfaction. 'If I'd known that was what I'd needed to jolt me out of my misery, I'd have had it years ago. Mind, it's a bit hard to find. Mind-blowing sex, that is.'

'I wouldn't know,' he said faintly.

'You don't know how hard it is to find? You haven't been looking?'

'Ginny…'

Her smile faded. 'It was fantastic,' she said softly. 'And not just the sex. Thank you, Fergus.'

'You're thanking me?'

'I surely am.'

'For what?'

'For jolting me.'

'I thought…what we had…it was more a joining than a jolting,' he said, cautious again.

She thought about that, considering it from all sides. 'You mean, joining in more than a sexual way?'

'I haven't always been celibate in the six years since my wife left,' he told her. 'But last night was different.'

'Mind-blowing.' The smugness was back.

He smiled, but persevered. 'Ginny, you and I could have something special. We do have something special. I feel it.'

'As in?' she whispered.

He hesitated but it may as well be said. It was how he was

feeling. 'There's no need for us to be alone,' he said. 'Just because we've been wounded in the past.'

'No,' she whispered. She stared out at the dogs, but the dogs were doing nothing, going nowhere. 'I figured that last night. I'd always thought…well, you know I'm a carrier for cystic fibrosis.'

'That doesn't mean you'll have children with cystic fibrosis.'

'No,' she agreed. Her tone was blank, almost businesslike. 'That would only happen if my partner is also a carrier. But even if my partner was free, I still have a fifty per cent chance of passing on carrier status to a child.'

'So?'

'So this damnable disease would live on through me. I've always sworn that will never happen.'

That was fine as far as it went, he thought. He nodded. 'There's life without children.'

'There is,' she said, and her voice softened. 'You'd know that all too well.'

'We could make it happen.' He couldn't stop the urgency entering his voice. He'd seen a glimpse of an escape—a sliver of something that might be a way of life he could embrace. A beautiful woman, smart and funny, a professional colleague with a life of her own. Someone who'd make him smile, who'd lie in his arms at night and take the emptiness away.

'I'm keeping the dogs,' she said, and his vision took a back step.

'That's crazy.'

'What's crazy about giving dogs a home?'

'We'd never be able to keep them.'

'We?'

'If you and I…'

'Fergus…'

'I'm just thinking, Ginny,' he said. 'I… Last night… You and I… For the first time since my wife left I thought that I might have met someone I could make a future with.' He lifted her hand, linking her fingers through his. 'Ginny, it was, as you said, mind-blowing. It made me think that maybe we could make something for ourselves. Be selfish. Just…put away the pain and create a partnership that would edge out the darkness.'

'Forget the darkness?' she whispered. 'How can we forget?'

'Block it out.'

'You can't do that,' she said softly. 'I've been running for years and it doesn't work. That's what I figured last night. I lay there after you left and I stared at the darkness and I thought the way I've been trying to block out the pain is by pretending to be someone I'm not. And I can't do that. I've been trying but it doesn't work. I'm just me. Ginny. And I need people. You made me see that last night.'

'You need me?' he asked, not understanding, and she shook her head.

'Not just you. Though you're definitely in there if you want to be in.'

'Gee, thanks.'

She smiled but her smile was troubled. 'Don't thank me, Fergus, because I don't think you want what I'm offering.'

'What are you offering?'

'I'm keeping the dogs,' she whispered.

He stared out at the canine pack. 'Why?'

'They'll be great when I've trained them.'

'You can't keep them in your Sydney apartment.'

'No.' Flat. Definite. Resolute.

'You're not seriously thinking about staying here.'

'No.' Her chin jutted a little and he thought he could see a trace of fear. She might be determined but this determination was very new and very…scary. 'I'm not thinking about staying here. I've decided to stay here.'

'After Richard…' He hesitated and glanced toward the bed.

'After Richard dies,' she said, and her voice steadied. 'I talked it through with Richard this morning and I have his blessing.'

'To do what?

'To make this house a home again,' she said. 'If I can. To give Madison a place to live.'

'You'll stay at Cradle Lake with Madison?' He forgot to whisper. If he sounded astounded, he couldn't help it. This was a woman whom he'd thought was running from commitment as fiercely as he was.

'I thought I hated it,' she whispered. 'Cradle Lake was claustrophobic. I knew everyone and everyone knew me. You know how many times I've had to cook since people found out Richard was back?'

'I don't—'

'I haven't had to,' she continued, ignoring his interruption. 'I've been away for almost fifteen years yet I'm still one of them. I have a community.'

He flinched.

A community.

'I have that where I work,' he said. 'It's not so rare. People care. It's why I'm here. To get away from it.'

'Yeah, but you've only been running for months. I've been running for fifteen years,' she whispered. 'I thought last night…I can stop.'

'Do you have any idea what you're saying?'

'I have,' she said, and again her chin jutted forward. He could see fear behind her eyes, he thought, and he knew she wasn't as determined as she made out. 'I'm jumping into the human race again. I thought…after I lost Richard that that'd be the end. It's not. It can't be and for some reason last night made me see that I don't want it to be. I don't want to hand Madison over to adoptive parents. Madison's my last link with my family and I want to teach her to use a canoe on the lake.'

'I could be your family,' he said, suddenly urgent, and she gazed down at their linked hands and her smile became almost wistful.

'You felt it, too, then. Last night.'

'I surely did.'

'More than mind-blowing sex.'

'Ginny, we fit together.'

'You and your wife,' she said cautiously. 'Did you fit?'

'It's different. We were professional, and our sole mutual interest was our work.'

'So you and me…what would our sole mutual interest be?'

'Ourselves,' he said, but it sounded lame even to him.

'I bet that's what you and your wife thought at the start. Fergus, I want something more from a relationship than a mutual involvement in medicine.'

He paused. Out in the pen one of the dogs, the collie, rolled over on her belly and started to scratch in an entirely undignified manner.

'This isn't what you were saying last night,' he said cautiously and she nodded.

'No. It's not. But I made you no promises last night, Fergus. I went into last night thinking it was a one-night stand and I can't help that it changed things.'

'What changed things?'

'You see, I don't know,' she whispered. 'I'm still trying to figure it out. I only know that I woke up different. I don't even know what's different.'

'Ginny, I want you.'

'That's lovely,' she said. 'I want you, too, Fergus. But I come with strings.'

'Dogs.'

'And a daughter.'

'You're not serious about Madison?'

'I've never been more serious.'

'She's damaged. She needs specialist care.'

'You think I can't give her that?'

'She needs two parents.' He spoke more roughly than he'd intended and both of them turned to look at Richard's bed. But Richard wasn't moving.

'I can't help that,' Ginny said apologetically. 'I only know that when I woke up this morning she was mine. I went to sleep in your arms last night thinking I had no family at all and when I woke up I did have family and I'll fight to the death to defend it.'

He stared at her, baffled. How could things have changed

so fast? He'd driven out here thinking that his world was starting to make sense again—just a bit. That he could find a little joy.

But Ginny wasn't content with a little joy. She wanted the whole catastrophe.

He stared out at the disreputable dogs and thought, Could he? Could he?

The screen door swung wide and out came Tony, who was carrying Madison, who was carrying a plate of cookies with exorbitant care.

'I didn't spill any of them,' Madison said, and Ginny beamed and bounced up and took the biscuits.

'That's brilliant, poppet,' she said, and Madison frowned.

'My name's Madison.'

'Yes, but you're also a poppet,' Ginny said. 'That's because you look very, very cute. I had a little brother like you once and my mum used to call him poppet.'

'Ginny,' Fergus said, almost explosively.

'Would you like a cookie, Dr Reynard?'

'No.' He took a grip—almost. The sight of Madison smiling was suddenly almost overwhelming. The pain...

Ginny saw it. Her face softened and she took a step toward him. 'Fergus, I'm sorry,' she murmured. 'I know it's much too soon.'

'It's never going to be any better,' he muttered, backing off. 'Is there anything else you need—medically?'

She saw it and responded immediately, as if she'd expected no less. 'We need orders for an increase in morphine. Richard was unsettled last night and I promised him he needn't be tonight.'

'I'll write it up now.' He turned to Tony. 'Tony...'

'I'll take Madison down to talk to the dogs while you sort out medical needs,' Ginny told him, setting down the cookies and gathering her niece into her arms. 'You look after the medicine. I'm looking after my family.'

'Ginny...'

'That's the way it has to be, Fergus,' she said softly. 'I knew when I figured it out last night that it wasn't going to be easy. I don't want to hurt you. But I know what I have to do.'

He couldn't do it.

Fergus drove away from the farmhouse feeling sick. He'd driven out here with his heart full of Ginny, feeling like he was waking from some sick, grey trance.

But now…

Dogs maybe. But Madison?

A little girl.

Like Molly.

She wasn't in the least like Molly, he thought savagely. She had all her chromosomes. She had a healthy heart. She could be a vibrant, happy little girl.

Ginny had no right to keep her. She needed two parents.

Molly had been OK with one parent. And the hospital community.

Madison was no Molly.

Molly.

The pain around his heart tightened, burned, threatened suddenly to almost overwhelm him. The thought of her small arms around his neck, the way she had of burrowing her nose into his shoulder and saying *Daddy, Daddy, Daddy,* like it was a mantra.

Madison wasn't burrowing her face into anyone's neck yet, he thought, but if she had proper parents she would be. She should be.

But it wouldn't be his.

No.

How could he lift a child and cuddle her and give her the love she deserved? He couldn't. Hell, it was hard enough caring for patients. It had been hard enough last night caring for Stephanie Horace. Stephanie was eight years old. She'd had to be admitted, and her father had a bad back. Fergus had carried her out to the car and even that had hurt. Having a child's body limp and warm against his chest.

What Ginny was asking was too much.

She wasn't asking it of him.

'Hell,' he said into the silence, and then he thumped the steering-wheel so hard that he hurt the back of his hand. 'Hell, hell, hell.'

Where were the answers?

There weren't any.

'Do you know what you're doing?'

Fergus had been gone for ten minutes. Ginny and Tony and Madison had consumed milk and cookies—or coffee and cookies for the grown-ups—and then Tony and Madison had gone inside to wash up. Soon Miriam would be there for handover.

They really didn't need a nurse here any more, Ginny thought as she sat on her veranda step and stared down over the lake. She'd agreed to a nurse being here because she hadn't wanted to get close to Madison, but now...

'He'll run a mile,' her brother whispered, and she turned to find Richard wide-eyed and watchful.

'You're awake.'

He managed a smile. 'Sometimes I can be.'

'How long have you been awake?' she asked cautiously, and he shrugged.

'Long enough to hear you scaring the good doctor into the middle of next week. He wants you, Ginny.'

'Maybe he does. But...'

'But what?'

'He doesn't want what comes with me.'

'Yesterday you had nothing,' Richard whispered. It was almost beyond him to speak now, and Ginny walked over and sat on his bed, taking his hand in hers, bending close so he didn't have to strain to speak. 'Yesterday you were running as fast as I have been.'

'Maybe we've both come to the end of our running.'

'I surely have,' he whispered. 'Hell, Ginny, you know it's OK with me if you have Madison adopted. We've asked so much of you. Big sister to a family of tragedy.'

'I loved you all,' she whispered back, speaking almost to herself. 'I loved Chris and Toby to bits. I loved Mum even when I knew she was drinking herself to death. I understood why you ran…'

'I behaved so unfairly. I wasn't so sick that I couldn't have helped.'

'No, but to watch what you'd have to go through yourself eventually…I understood.'

'Everyone has to die some time. I was just a coward. Like Dad was a coward. But not you. You were always the bravest, Ginny, and I'll not let you be taken advantage of. I'll organise Madison into foster-care myself.'

'You do so over my dead body,' she said, and her sudden flash of anger startled them both. 'She's my family.'

'We don't do family,' he whispered, but her fury was still there.

'Like hell we don't. Who did you come back to when you were ill?'

'That's different?'

'Why is it different? You know I slept with Fergus last night?'

'I guessed,' he said, and managed a wry smile. 'Was it good?'

She smiled back, aware that her face was flushed but also knowing that there wasn't a thing she could do about it.

'It was excellent. The thing is…'

'The thing is, what?' he asked, closing his eyes and she withdrew her hand from his.

'You're so tired. I shouldn't—'

'I have all the time in the world for sleeping,' he said, and the anger was in his voice now. He left his eyes closed but his hand still held hers. 'The thing is, what?'

'I fell in love,' she said softly, and his eyes flew open again.

'You fell in love.'

'Just like that,' she whispered. 'And he left—he had a house call—and I lay there and I thought I've been trying to seal up the jagged edges. Every time there's a death… Chris, Toby, Mum and now you… It hurts so much and I've been trying to shrink my heart, make it less and less exposed. And it's been grey and horrid and I didn't know what to do about it except to keep on shrinking. Only then, this morning, suddenly all those jagged edges opened up again and it was like my heart was suddenly…beating again.'

'Oh, Ginny…'

'It feels better,' she said, almost defiantly. 'Sure, it's crazy—it's terrifying if you like, but the alternative's worse. You've had fun since you've been diagnosed. You've had lovers. The result of one of them is in our kitchen eating cookies right now. But you always knew you were going to die. It didn't stop you learning to surf, seeing every part of Australia you could, having fun…'

'Yes, but…'

'But that's what I'm saying,' she whispered. 'It's the same thing. I figured it last night. Yeah, I might get hurt again but if I don't take those risks then I might as well wither right now. So I'm taking on the dogs and I'm taking on Madison.'

'And Fergus?'

She hesitated. 'He has his own figuring out to do,' she whispered.

'He's been hurt?'

'He's lost a child. Recently.'

'A little girl.'

'Mmm.'

'Then it's not fair to ask him to take on Madison.'

'It's not,' she agreed. 'And I'm not asking him to.'

'But you want her.'

'I'll fight to the death to keep her.'

'Even if it means losing Fergus.'

'I don't think I can lose Fergus,' she whispered. 'I don't think I have him to lose.'

'He loves you.'

'I don't think he's figured what love really is,' she said. 'What it can be.'

'So what will you do?'

'Take care of my brother for as long as he needs me,' she whispered, and stooped to kiss him lightly on the forehead.

'Look after three dogs. Look after one little girl. And…maybe even look after the medical needs of Cradle Lake. For as long as Cradle Lake will have me.'

CHAPTER NINE

RICHARD slept.

Miriam arrived to take over nursing duties from Tony. She didn't question the fact that there were now three dogs on the place, or that when she arrived Ginny was sitting under the trees with Madison. Heaven knew what Tony told her—probably every single damned thing, including her thoughts, Ginny thought, but she didn't think it bitterly. Cradle Lake had seemed a prison for years. The community's intimate knowledge of everyone's nearest concerns had seemed claustrophobic. Now, suddenly, it seemed like a refuge.

'You know, Madison's a very long name,' she told her niece cautiously as they finished the third reading of 'A Poky Little Puppy'. Did your mummy call you Madison all the time?'

'My mummy says Madison's a lovely name,' the child whispered. She was lying on the grass beside Ginny. When they'd first started telling stories Madison had been a good foot away. But then one of the dogs—the whippet—had crawled over to drape herself over Ginny's stomach and Madison had come a little closer when Ginny had encouraged her to pat the dog, and now the child's little body was hard against Ginny's. It was a tiny measure of trust but it made Ginny feel...well, that maybe things could work. That maybe things were working. For her as well as for Madison.

'Did she ever call you Maddy?'

'Only when she was giggly,' Madison said.

'Was she often giggly?'

'My mummy stopped being giggly,' Madison whispered. 'She says the pills took away her giggle. She used to cry.'

'Sometimes it's right to cry,' Ginny said, stroking the little girl's tousled curls. 'Sometimes it's the only way to say goodbye to people. I think your mummy was crying because she knew she was saying goodbye to you.'

'I didn't want her to go.'

'No, but when something's so wrong that even the doctors can't make it right then there's no choice. Your mummy would have stayed with you if she could, but she was too sick. Instead, she brought you here. To be with your daddy for a little bit, to get to know him until he has to say goodbye. Then to be with me. And Miriam and Tony and all these lazy, lazy dogs...'

The whippet chose that moment to turn and give Ginny a slurpy kiss. I hope she's been wormed, Ginny thought, and then decided there was no way Oscar would have wormed his dogs but maybe worms were the least of their problems.

But she'd worm dogs and everyone associated with dogs right away. A nice uncomplicated piece of medicine.

'Will we stay here for ever?' Madison asked, and Ginny stroked her hair some more.

'Would you like to?'

'I'd rather stay with my mummy.'

'You know you can't do that. But me and the dogs might learn to be OK. You might get to like us.' She stroked the child's curls some more, fighting for the right words. 'Your mummy and your daddy have been unlucky,' she said at last. 'I think you won't have to say goodbye to me for a very long time. So far ahead you can't even imagine.'

Was it the right thing? 'Mmm,' Madison said noncommittally, but her head stayed on Ginny's lap and she snoozed into sleep. Ginny gazed up and saw that Miriam had been standing on the back step, listening. She wiped her eyes fiercely with the back of her hand, said, 'Dratted hayfever,' and disappeared into the house with speed.

Hayfever was catching. Ginny found herself sniffing and hauled herself together with a fierceness that was almost anger.

She'd lose Richard.

Did she have to lose Fergus?

Slowly the anger faded. She stared out over the sleepy rural landscape and tried to do a bit of crystal-ball gazing. Which was very, very hard.

For no matter how she looked, the crystal ball didn't show Fergus.

Her heart was screaming *Fergus*.

If she went back to the city she could be with him. Maybe it could work. Her hands were stroking Madison's hair and the whippet was nuzzling her leg. If she went back to the city then maybe…maybe a suburban block…

No. Fergus wanted no appendages. He'd made that clear. Even looking at Madison hurt. He wanted a sexy relationship with no strings.

Yesterday that had been fine but now… She wanted strings. She was desperate for strings, and here they were lying on her lap. She was damned if she'd cut any more strings of her own accord.

'I'm calling you Twiggy Two after my old dog,' she told the whippet. Then, as the other two dogs thought maybe this wasn't a trap and maybe they, too, could get into this patting business, she granted them names as well. 'You're Snapper,' she told the collie, and the collie snapped at a fly in honour of the naming ceremony. 'And you're Bounce,' she told the little dog. 'Because I'm betting that if I feed you right and hug you often, that's what you'll do. Like Madison… By the time I finish with her, she'll be Maddy. You mark my words.'

It'd be OK. She was sure it'd be OK.

'Phone,' Miriam said from the veranda, and she sounded apologetic, as if she knew how important this discussion was and she really didn't want to interrupt it. She still sounded sniffy. 'It's Fergus. He needs you.'

No, he doesn't, Ginny thought but she handed over her charges to Miriam and went to find what the impersonal need was that Fergus wanted her for.

'Ginny, Stephanie Horace has appendicitis. She's the eight-year-old I admitted this morning with suspected gastro. The symptoms this morning weren't specific but they are now. Can you give the anaesthetic if I operate straight away?'

Fergus's voice was so formal that she almost flinched. Instead, she held the phone away from her face, took a deep breath and switched into medical mode. Or tried to. She wasn't too sure how she'd handle being close to Fergus right now.

It'd be easier if they didn't have to see each other, she thought bleakly, but she still needed his help with Richard, and she had agreed to help him when needed.

'You're sure it's appendicitis?' she asked, without much hope.

'There was very little local tenderness this morning, plus there was a history of two siblings with a tummy bug a couple of days before.' Fergus sounded more strained than the situation demanded. Maybe he was feeling the same as she was. 'I popped her into hospital with an IV line and she settled, but she's started vomiting again now. There's acute tenderness on the right side and she's looking sick.'

'You're thinking that an attack of gastro could have pushed a grumbling appendix into an acute infection,' Ginny said, and got a grunt of assent.

'That's what it looks like. No rebound yet but I want it out fast. Can you help or will I send her on?'

Rebound pain—pain when pressure was released—was a sign of a burst appendix. If there was no rebound pain they might be in time to take out an intact appendix. Much as she didn't want to face Fergus again so soon, there was no choice. 'Of course I'll help.'

'I thought you might not…'

Oh, for heaven's sake… If she could be clinical, surely he could be, too. 'You thought I might not what?' she snapped.

'You offered to help out before,' he said. 'But things have changed. You're making a family.'

'Yes, things have changed.' Her voice softened. 'Fergus, there's no either-or in this game. You're saying I'm an un-emotional clinical medico or I'm part of a family? I'm allowed to be both. You were both until Molly died. I'm both now.' She looked down at her torn jeans with dog hair attached and grimaced. 'Look out for the lady with so much domesticity attached to her you can't imagine. That'll be me. But I'm also a doctor. Have the theatre ready the minute I arrive.'

'That's telling him,' Miriam said mildly as Ginny put down the phone, and Ginny turned and faced her with a slightly shamefaced smile.

'I had no business talking to him like that. But he was being…'

'Ridiculous?' Miriam smiled back at her. 'Maybe he is. He's in love with you, Ginny.'

'No, he's not.'

'Are you crazy? He can't keep his eyes off you. Richard and I were just saying so. The man's besotted.'

'He's not in love with me. How can he be? His little girl died three months ago. He's raw with pain.'

'Oh, my dear,' Miriam said softly, her smile fading. 'We did wonder. Is that why he came here? To get away?'

'Apparently.'

'That makes it so much harder. Now you're taking on the little one.'

'I know,' she whispered. 'But how can I not? You know our family history. Madison looks like Toby. She looks like Chris. How can I not be part of her family? I just…am.'

'Even if it means giving up Dr Reynard.'

'I don't have him to give up,' she said honestly. 'He fancies me as an unencumbered partner when needed, but it seems en-cumbrances are part of who I am. I just seem to collect them.'

'And if he loves you then he has to see the whole picture,' Miriam agreed. 'Encumbrances included.'

'Like that's going to happen. I don't think so.'

The appendix burst just as Fergus reached it. 'Damn,' he muttered and glanced up to see that she'd realised what had happened. A straightforward appendectomy took only minutes and Ginny had administered a really light anaesthetic. Now that it had burst there needed to be a full washout of the cavity, carefully cleaning every possible trace of the infected tissue.

Ginny nodded and adjusted her dosage, then went back to watching her dials, monitoring breathing, taking care...

But Stephanie was a normally, healthy eight-year-old who'd only been ill for twelve hours. This was not a complicated anaesthetic. There was time to watch Fergus operate, to see the skill in his fingers, to think that he couldn't be expected to stay here.

With a skill like this, he should be a city surgeon.

So what was she about, wanting him to stay here?

She didn't want him to stay here.

She didn't want to stay here herself. But she would. Madison needed her. The dogs needed her.

She needed to be needed.

'Oscar's heard you've taken his dogs.' Mary, the nurse assisting Fergus, handed Fergus his threaded needle. The cleaning was finished and Fergus was starting to close. The nurse went back to swabbing to keep the site clear of blood but she was relaxed enough now to talk to Ginny. Mary was an older nurse than Miriam, another farmer's wife. Her farm was just north of Oscar's. 'He's telling everyone it's theft and he's talking about having you arrested,' she said.

'He's angry about everything,' Fergus muttered, concentrating on stitching. 'The man's perpetually twisted. You want me to kick him out of the nursing home and tell him to go and look after his dogs himself?'

'He'd die,' Ginny said, but there was a certain amount of reluctance in her voice. Fergus glanced up at her.

'And you wouldn't be sorry?'

'I'm always sorry when patients pass on,' she said, and made her voice prim. 'But those dogs have been starved and beaten. It's a wonder the whole six of them aren't savage.'

'He's not happy in the nursing home,' Mary said, threading the next needle.

'Tell me where he would be happy.'

'He's never had a family,' Mary said. 'What he needed was a wife and six kids. Instead, he's just sat in that farmhouse and thought about the injustices of the world. Until he's come to this.'

That caused a bit of an extended silence where Mary appeared to think about what she'd said.

'I mean, there's nothing wrong with not being married,' she said at last, a trifle self-consciously. 'I dare say you two will turn out to be very nice people.'

Fergus grinned. 'Not me. I'm into injustices. Like Ginny being arrested for taking on the care of three starved dogs. That could get me bitter and twisted in no time.'

'Then you'll be carted off to a nursing home, kicking and screaming,' Ginny retorted. 'Any minute now. Get yourself some encumbrances.'

'There's three of Oscar's dogs left,' he said thoughtfully. 'Maybe I should take them on.'

'The ranger put them down this morning,' Mary said, and all their smiles faded.

'With Oscar's permission?' Fergus asked.

'Oscar said put them all down,' Mary told them. 'Including the ones Ginny has. He's decided to come into the nursing home and he doesn't want anyone benefiting from his animals. He's almost psychotic about being ripped off, so technically Ginny's guilty of dog-napping.'

'He's not happy that she's saved their lives?' Fergus demanded, incredulous, and Mary shook her head.

'I'll give the man enemas,' Fergus muttered. 'Three a day for as long as we both shall live.'

'You're only here for another ten weeks,' Mary reminded him, and he glowered some more.

'Time enough. That's seventy by three—two hundred and ten enemas. He'll crack and sign a promise not to sue before I'm done with him.'

'He won't sue,' Ginny said. 'The man's all bluster. I'm not frightened of him.'

'You used to be,' Mary retorted. 'He and your mother… that's an old story that Oscar will never let drop. There was a story went round the town when you were about eight—that Oscar berated your mother and you stood up for her. And he belted you. My uncle was the town policeman at the time and I remember him being livid that your mother wouldn't press charges.'

'He hit you?' Fergus demanded. He was concentrating on the job at hand, but it was merely dressing now and there was room for rage.

'He hit lots of things in his time,' Mary said equitably. 'But look at him now. Alone in a nursing home with his very own doctor threatening to give him enemas.'

'Which I'll thank you not to give him,' Ginny said equitably. 'That's all in the past now.'

'You've moved on.'

'As of last night I have—Doctor,' she said meekly, and both Mary and Fergus stared at her.

'You want me to reverse my anaesthetic?' she asked, and they were back into medical mode again. Which was just as well.

'Yes, please,' Fergus said, but Mary stared at both of them and Ginny thought, no, she hadn't moved on.

But Ginny wasn't answering questions. She couldn't.

Mary and a young orderly took the recovering Stephanie out of Theatre. Fergus left to let the parents know how things had gone. Ginnie rid herself of her theatre gear fast, hoping to escape, but when she emerged Fergus was seated in the waiting room with a couple who were obviously Stephanie's parents.

The woman had been crying, Ginny saw, and it was obviously taking time to reassure her and to be able to speak coherently to the pair of them.

'The appendix has burst,' he was saying. 'It's out now and it's fine, but it was a bit messy. I'm really sorry I didn't diagnose it this morning. It's meant that we need to keep Stephanie in hospital for a little longer than we otherwise would. She'll have to stay on intravenous antibiotics to make sure the infection from the appendix doesn't cause any more problems.'

'But she will be OK?' the woman asked tremulously, and Fergus met her look square on. He hesitated, but the woman was shaking. He put a hand on her shoulder and gripped, hard.

It was often like this with people who'd never had medical trauma in their lives before, Ginny thought. These two had been shocked to the core by the realisation that their little girl was vulnerable in the worst possible way.

To lose a child…

Fergus had lost a child. What that must mean…

'She'll be OK,' he was saying.

Ginny should go through the room, past them to the exit. At the very least she should make her presence felt. Instead, she stood in the doorway and watched.

'If you'd operated earlier, it wouldn't have burst,' the farmer said, probing, and Fergus nodded.

'That's right. It was my mistake and I'm sorry for it.'

How often did you hear a doctor say that? Ginny thought incredulously. Surgeons had a reputation for being mini-gods in their domain.

Not this one.

'But we all thought it was gastro.' The woman was crying still, but she'd calmed down now and she took Fergus's hand and lifted it. 'The local school…one kid after another has gone down with this bug and we thought it was the same. We practically told you it was the same. And Clive here even thought you were overreacting when you brought her in this morning. Bloody doctors trying to fill hospital beds, he said, and I agreed. So...' She gulped. 'So I'm saying there's no blame on you from us for not diagnosing it earlier. Is there, Clive?' And she turned to her husband and waited.

Hmm.

It could go either way here, Ginny thought. Clive Horace had the look of a man who could be belligerent.

But it seemed that Fergus's blatant apology had done the trick.

'We won't be blaming you, Doc,' he said. 'If you hadn't been here and she stopped vomiting, we probably wouldn't have even taken her to the doctor until late today 'cos it'd mean a three-hour drive. By which time I reckon she'd be worse.'

'She would have been.'

'Just lucky you were here, then,' he said, and he looked up and saw Ginny watching. 'And you, too, miss,' he told her. 'The nurse said you'd given the anaesthetic. And you a Viental and all.'

'I—'

'Your family's had such rotten luck,' the farmer said. 'And here we are, terrified about one of our kidlets with appendicitis. I don't know what we're making a fuss about.'

'If it was my kid, I'd be making a fuss,' Ginny said.

'They say you have a kid,' the farmer said. 'Richard's kid. They say you're taking her on.'

'I... Yes.'

'You're a brave lass.' He rose and took his wife's hand, drawing her up after him. 'Thanks to you both,' he said heavily. 'Can we see her now?'

She wanted to go home. She felt drained and a little sick. She turned and headed out to the car park and when she heard Fergus, call she was tempted not to stop.

'Ginny.'

She did stop but she didn't turn to face him. She just stood motionless, staring ahead at her car.

He caught her and touched her shoulder. She flinched. She'd made her decision—but she didn't have to like it.

He withdrew his hands. 'Ginny?'

'Yes?'

'I was wondering if you'd come out with me tonight.'

'I don't think that's a good idea.'

'No,' he said gravely. 'It's a dumb idea. But it's the only idea I have. Hell, Ginny, what sort of a childhood did you have?'

'Are you saying you want to take me out tonight because you feel sorry for me?' she managed, and she heard him suck in his breath in exasperation.

'Of course not.'

'Then what?'

'I just think you're the bravest woman,' he murmured. 'I've never met anyone like you. Ginny, I really need to get to know you better.'

'I don't think that's a good idea either.'

'Why not?'

She whirled to face him. 'Because I'm falling in love with you,' she whispered.

'I think that's a really good idea,' he said, and he smiled.

'No, it's not.'

'Ginny, we need to see where this can take us.'

'That's nuts. Like there's five roads branching out ahead and we know three end in brick walls, so let's just put our foot on the accelerator and go where the steering-wheel takes us.'

'I just want to take you to dinner.'

'No.'

'Why not?'

'You know why not.'

'Richard's doing little but sleeping. Miriam's with Madison…'

'You see, there's the problem,' she whispered. 'Madison needs to be with me. She needs to start seeing me as a constant.'

He drew in his breath at that. He really was absurdly handsome, Ginny thought inconsequentially. He was still wearing his theatre gown and slippers, hospital green. He'd raked his hair as he'd spoken to Stephanie's parents and it was tousled and rumpled and she just want to…

No!

'Maybe I could try,' he said, and she blinked.

'Try. Try what?'

He chewed his bottom lip. 'Ginny, this thing between us… You say you think you're falling in love.'

'I'm trying very hard not to,' she said, and he nodded.

'Me, too.'

'So why are you asking me out to dinner?'

'Because I've got this appalling feeling that I might be making a mistake.'

'Fergus, my appendages aren't going to go away,' she said softly. 'Believe me, I didn't mean this to happen. I know, this is really fast but it's overwhelming. Every time I look at you I think how can I have appendages when it means I can't have you? But I do have them, Fergus. Madison is right here in my heart and I'm even falling for my dogs.'

'OK, then,' he said, and she blinked again.

'OK, what?'

'I'll try.'

'You'll try what?'

'Let's have a picnic on the lake tonight. With appendages attached.'

'Not in the boatshed,' she said in a hurry, and he grinned.

'Not in the boatshed.'

'A proper picnic.' She sounded suspicious but she couldn't help it.

'Yes.'

She bit her lip but it had to be said. 'I can bring Madison?'

'You can bring anyone you want.'

'A barbecue.'

'Yes. If we can build one on the shore.'

'There's a cairn down on the east shore we can use as a barbecue.' She stared at him for a long moment and came to a decision. 'Right. If I leave now, I can catch the butcher.'

'Just like that?'

'Just like that,' she said. 'Are you doing evening surgery?'

'Yes, but it's lightly booked. It should be finished by six.'

'I'll see you at seven, then,' she told him. 'On the east shore. With sausages.'

'See you then.'

Terrific, she thought as she drove butcher-wards. What on earth was she doing?

She didn't have a clue.

CHAPTER TEN

SHE was there—with appendages. Fergus pulled into the east shore parking area, where a row of eucalypts divided the paddocks from the sandy shore, and he thought she'd brought everyone she could think of.

Ginny. Madison. Twiggy, Snapper and Bounce. Richard, lying on a blow-up mattress on the shoreline and seemingly asleep, and Miriam, calmly sitting beside him, her stockings off and her feet in the water.

It was a real family picnic, Fergus thought, and he wanted to run.

'Hi.' Ginny rose from where she'd been sorting through a picnic hamper. She was wearing a crimson bikini with a crimson and white sarong. She was smiling.

Maybe he didn't want to run.

'Bounce nearly ate the sausages,' Madison announced. She was also wearing a bikini—a miniature version of Ginny's. The Cradle Lake ladies auxiliary had held a working bee to augment Madison's scant wardrobe. She now had outfits for every occasion, but her tiny body still looked waiflike and Fergus felt his heart wrench.

Maybe he should run.

'So who saved the sausages?' he asked, and Richard opened his eyes and managed a weary smile.

'Our Ginny was a rugby player in a previous life. It was a tackle that would have done an international player proud.'

'Ginny got a sore knee,' Madison said gravely, and Fergus looked at said knee and saw a graze and a trace of blood.

'Do you need a doctor?' he asked, and she flushed a little.

'I don't need a doctor, thank you very much,' she managed.

'We need a cook,' Miriam told him. 'You're on barbecue duty.'

'Why?'

'Men tend barbecues,' Richard whispered. 'And I can't.'

It was all Richard could do to make himself heard, Fergus thought, looking down at his patient in concern. It must have cost him a huge effort to be there tonight. But together Miriam and Ginny had him comfortable. They had his oxygen cylinder set just above the water line. They'd lain him right on the water's edge and he had a hand trailing lazily in the water.

The night was warm and dreamy, the sun a low ball of fading heat, reflecting softly off the water. If I only had a few days left, this is where I might like to be, Fergus thought, and glanced at Ginny and saw she was thinking exactly what he was thinking. There was pain behind her eyes, knowledge of imminent loss.

'Let's get these sausages cooked,' he said, maybe more roughly than he'd intended. 'Maddy, would you like to help me?'

'Madison,' she whispered.

'Sorry. Madison, would you, please, help me with the sausages?'

'What do you want me to do?'

'Have they been pricked?'

'Pricked?'

'No,' Ginny told him. 'They're unpricked sausages.'

'That's a terrible state of affairs,' he told the little girl. 'Let me teach you how to professionally prick a sausage.'

They pricked, cooked and ate their sausages. They polished off salad and lamingtons and sponge cake and grapes and lemonade.

'It's time to swim,' Ginny decreed.

'Aren't you supposed to wait for half an hour after eating?' Fergus asked, and she gazed at him blankly.

'Why?'

'In case of cramp.'

'What medical textbook did that come out of?'

'My mother's,' he said, and she grinned.

'My mother said every minute out of the water on a night like this was a minute wasted. Are you pitting your mother against my mother?'

'No,' he said faintly. 'I daren't.'

'You did bring your togs?'

He had. He felt a bit self-conscious hauling off his shirt and trousers, with everyone looking at him. Ginny had seen him before but the thought of that made him even more self-conscious—and Miriam whistling didn't help at all.

'Ooh, Dr Fergus. You make me go all wobbly round the knees.'

'I begin to see what you see in the man,' Richard managed, and Fergus made a valiant attempt not to blush.

'I'm swimming,' he said, and turned toward the water.

'Not before the race,' Ginny announced, and he hesitated.

'The race?'

'We have a boat.' Ginny gestured up the bank to where an ancient bathtub lay on its side.

'That's a bathtub,' he said cautiously.

'The man's intelligent as well as good-looking,' Richard whispered. 'Ginny, you've struck gold.'

'Quiet,' Ginny ordered. She turned back to the lake and gestured to a series of poles curving about two hundred yards out into the lake. 'We use the bath to paddle through as many poles as we can. The poles are all in shallow water,' she said. 'They mark the boundary of where non-swimmers can go. Plus they act as a sort of slalom run.'

'A slalom run,' Fergus said cautiously. 'As in skiing. Right. Um… Anything else I should know?'

'Our bathtub doesn't have a plug.'

'Right.'

Ginny grinned at his evident confusion. 'Right behind where the bath is, there's a clay bank,' she told him. 'It's really gluey clay, and it's the makings of a Cradle Lake tradition. You make your own plug. Your plug can be made of anything you can find on the ground, like leaves, grass, even cow pats—but the plug has to be held together by clay.'

'I see.' He shook his head. 'Nope. I don't see.'

'The trick is to make your plug, launch your bath and then paddle—using only arms over the side. You weave in and out of the poles. The record is the third last marker before the plug disintegrates and the bath sinks.'

'Who holds the record?' Fergus asked, and Richard managed a smile.

'That would be me. Aged all of fourteen. Twenty-three poles.'

'Richard was great,' Ginny told them, smiling down at her brother in affection. 'But, Fergus, you're a grown man with muscles that make even Miriam whistle. Surely you can beat a mere fourteen-year-old whippersnapper.'

'With cystic fibrosis,' Richard added. 'Everyone without cystic fibrosis should be handicapped.'

'No one's beaten your record,' Ginny said soundly. 'Stuff cystic fibrosis. It didn't beat you then.'

It didn't beat you then...

This was a battle, Fergus thought. He looked from brother to sister and back again and thought this disease had been a part of their lives for so long that it was a tangible thing. A monster to be beaten, over and over again.

Until it could no longer be beaten. Which would be soon.

Meanwhile, they were watching him. Expectant.

'You want me to show you how it's done?' Ginny asked. 'Richard would but he's a bit tied up at the moment.'

'You could say that,' Richard said, and grinned. 'Madison, sit by me while your Aunty Ginny plays boat captain.'

'I reckon Madison could go in the boat,' Miriam said, smiling at the lot of them like an indulgent aunt instead of the efficient nurse she was.

'Can the dogs go in the boat, too?' Madison asked, and Ginny held up her hands in horror.

'One child maybe but no dogs. I intend to set a mark that

Dr Reynard can't beat. Madison, you can help paddle but the dogs would sink us by the first pole.'

'Right,' Miriam said decisively. 'That's it, then. The crews are decided. Let's get this boat race under way.'

It looked easy, Fergus thought, sitting on the sun-warmed sand and waiting as Ginny prepared her plug.

'The trick is not to show Dr Reynard what we're doing,' she told Madison, and they turned their backs on him and stooped over the clay bank. 'But the trick is to weave the grass, over and over. Watch.'

Two heads bent, intent.

This was great, Fergus thought. This, for Madison, was a night off. She was totally absorbed, and for the moment she could forget the horrors of abandonment, the loss of her mother. She was handing Ginny blade after blade of grass, and a complicated piece of neurosurgery couldn't have elicited more attention.

'Right,' said Ginny at last. 'Fergus, you're permitted to help haul the bath to the water's edge.'

'Gee, thanks.'

'Think nothing of it.'

They hauled the bath down to the shore, then Ginny fitted the now empty picnic hamper into the rear, upside down.

'That's your seat,' she told Madison. 'Put your toes down into the water and kick as hard as you can. Kick and kick and kick. I find yelling helps, too. A sort of warrior war cry. Listen as I yell and follow.'

Madison looked dubiously at Ginny. For a moment Fergus thought she'd refuse, but Ginny was squeezing a little more water out of her plug and not paying attention.

Finally she looked up, satisfied.

'Right,' she told Madison, woman to woman. 'Are we ready?'

'Yes,' said Madison.

So Madison was seated on the wicker basket. Ginny climbed aboard and squished her plug into the hole.

'Right,' she yelled. 'Push.'

Fergus and Miriam pushed the boat out into the water, through the first poles.

'Go,' Ginny yelled. She was in the bow of the bath, leaning forward so her hands were paddling crazily in front of her. The boat was hardly steerable. The trick was to get close enough to the next pole to grab it and haul the tub around. 'Go, go go,' Ginny yelled, and Madison kicked with a ferocity that belied her four years of age.

'Go,' Madison yelled, entering into the spirit of things and kicking harder. 'Go, go, go.'

The dogs were going crazy, barking in chorus. Miriam was laughing, and Richard was doing a close approximation to a chuckle, holding his hands up and clapping to show encouragement.

Five poles. Six. Seven, eight…

The tub settled lower in the water.

'Kick,' Ginny yelled, hauling the tub round the next pole. 'Go, go go.'

Two more poles. The bow dipped…

The bathtub slid silently underwater, but by the time it sank Ginny had Madison in her arms, hugging her and cheering as their vessel disappeared from view.

'We were fantastic, Maddy, girl,' she whooped. 'Weren't we fantastic?'

'Madison,' Maddy said, but she was smiling.

'Fourteen poles,' Ginny said in satisfaction. 'Beat that, Dr Reynard.'

Only, of course, he couldn't. He made a plug he was sure would hold. Miriam and Ginny and Madison shoved him forward with a push he had to concede was as powerful a start as he'd given them. They whooped, the dogs barked—and he sank as he reached the eleventh pole.

'Pathetic,' Richard whispered as they hauled the bathtub back to shore. 'See what cystic fibrosis can do for a man?'

'I'll get better,' Fergus said.

'Not if you only stay here a few more weeks,' Richard told him. 'It takes a lifetime to build a skill like that.'

He broke off, gasping, and Ginny flinched. But it seemed she was determined to keep them all cheerful.

'We all need a swim,' she said determinedly. 'Richard, would you like us to push you further in?'

'I'm happy where I am,' Richard managed. 'Just watching. I've pushed my bathtub for twenty-three poles. What more can a man expect out of life?'

They stayed until dark. Miraculously Fergus's pager stayed silent. They dried off. Ginny did a quick change behind a beach towel that had Fergus fascinated. Then they toasted marshmallows on the fire and sat and watched as the moon came up over the water.

Miriam excused herself. 'I'll be back at the house when you get there,' she told them, 'but there's not a lot of nursing to be done here. Fergus, if you'll stay to help Ginny get them all home, I might nip home myself and spend an hour or two watering my vegetable patch.'

'She shouldn't be staying with us,' Ginny said, obviously feeling guilty as Miriam left.

'It's cost-effective,' Fergus told her. 'We worked it out. Two patients needing full-time care. We'd have to put another nurse on if we had them in hospital so the board's happy to pay Tony and Miriam and Bridget to work like this.'

'How hard did you have to twist their arms?'

'I didn't,' Fergus said honestly. 'This is a great little community, Ginny.'

'I know it is,' she said. 'I hadn't realised... If only my parents had asked for help...'

'And you hadn't had a neighbour like Oscar.'

She shrugged. 'Oscar's irrelevant.' She turned and looked at Richard. As the sun had set they'd piled blankets over him to keep him warm. He'd stayed awake until the last ray had faded behind the distant mountains, watching with something akin to greed.

He'd watched the sun set on the lake. He'd watched his daughter trying to swim.

This was some hospice, Fergus thought. Would that all dying patients got such care.

He was deeply asleep now. Deeply…

For a moment Fergus hesitated, but then he rose and crossed to the makeshift bed. He stooped and felt for the pulse.

It was still there. Just. A thready, too fast pattern.

He turned and Ginny was hugging Madison to her, tight. Her face had blenched.

'It's OK,' he said gently. 'He's still with us.'

The tension eased from her face, but not the pain.

'Soon,' she whispered.

'Soon,' he agreed. 'But you've given him this night. You've given him the knowledge that his little girl will be cared for. It's some gift, Ginny.'

'You've helped,' she whispered. Like Richard, Madison had slumped into sleep. She'd been seated beside Ginny and gradually she'd eased down onto Ginny's knees. Ginny was cradling her, taking comfort as well as giving it.

The little girl stirred now and whimpered a little, as if she realised that the arms she was in weren't those of her mother. Ginny eased her down onto the rug, pulling another rug over her. Then she sat and watched the tiny face, concentrating fiercely on sleep.

Soon they'd have to stir. They'd have to wake Richard and move him back to the house. Soon this evening would be ended.

She didn't want it to end, Fergus thought, watching Ginny's face and knowing instinctively what she was thinking. She knew her brother wouldn't be coming back here.

Something was ending tonight.

He couldn't bear it.

He didn't remember moving. He just…did. One minute he was kneeling beside Richard. The next minute he was on the rug with Ginny. He had her in his arms and he was kissing her.

He was kissing her as she needed to be kissed.

It was different from last night. Last night their love-making had been driven by passion and laughter and mutual need.

Tonight…

Tonight he needed to kiss this woman as he needed to breathe. She was so beautiful, so needful, so brave…

She was taking the world onto her shoulders and she'd already been there. He had no doubt of the childhood she'd had, loaded with responsibility beyond her years, and here she was taking it on all over again.

She was so…so…

Ginny.

And she needed him. He could feel it in the way her body melted into his. In the way her face came up to meet his kiss, but more. It was as if she was a part of him that he hadn't realised was missing. When her lips met his it was a completeness that he'd never experienced, could never experience with anyone but this woman.

Ginny.

Her lips were opening under his. She was wearing a fleecy jogging suit, soft pants and an oversized sweater, which should be keeping her warm on such a mild night and so close to the fire, but she was trembling.

He held her and kissed her and kissed her and he thought this was right, this was how the world was meant to be.

This woman in his arms for always. For ever.

But Madison's little body was hard pressed against Ginny. Maybe she felt the change in Ginny's body. Maybe she felt the trembling and it fed her own insecurities. For whatever reason, she suddenly whimpered a little and drew away.

It broke the moment. Ginny's hands touched his shoulders but already he was drawing away, looking down at the child in concern, looking back at Ginny, seeing Ginny's uncertainty in the firelight…

'I…' She reached up and touched her lips where she'd been kissed, as if she had trouble understanding the sensation, the taste, the lingering feeling of awe she must feel because that was how he felt. Like the world had changed.

She'd said their time in the boatshed had changed her world, he thought, dazed. Maybe…maybe tonight had changed his.

No. Last night he'd known that he wanted this woman. The only thing that had changed was the intensity of that feeling.

'Ginny, we need to be together,' he whispered, and touched her face.

'I don't see how.'

'We can work it out. We must.'

'I don't see how.'

'I can do this,' he said. He hesitated, taking in the scene lit by the firelight and the rising moon. A dying man. Three dogs, lying by Richard's side. Richard had demanded the leftover sausages and he'd fed pieces of them to the dogs while they'd swum, making them his devoted fans for ever. Or for however long he had.

Before him was a beautiful woman, huddled into an over-sized windcheater, gazing at him with eyes that were uncertain—but challenging. All or nothing, her gaze said. If I can do it, you can do it. Start again.

A child.

A little girl lying by her side.

He could do this. He could step back into...

'It's too soon, Fergus,' she said gently but surely. 'Molly's been dead only these last few months. It's too soon to even think you can create another family.'

'It's not replacing,' he said, but for the life of him he couldn't keep the uncertainty out of his voice. 'Molly and Madison...they're so different.'

'Yes, but—'

'I love you, Ginny,' he said. 'I'll do whatever it takes.'

'You see, that's what I don't want,' she whispered. 'Because I don't think that I'm even ready for that. Yesterday I thought that maybe I could rejoin the human race. I could let myself get attached to Madison and the dogs and this community. But taking you on...'

'What do you mean, taking me on?' he asked, startled, and she managed a wavering smile.

'You come with your own ghosts,' she said. 'If I didn't have a mass of my own to deal with then maybe I could help you with yours.'

'I'm not asking you to.'

'No. But…Fergus, I'm not denying this love thing…this feeling we have for each other. The way you make me feel. But it scares me. Everything scares me. Come back to me in a year or so when I've learned what loving is again. When you've figured out what it means not being Molly's dad any more.'

'Ginny, I want you.'

'I know. But we need to be sensible.'

'I don't feel like being sensible.' He touched her cheek with the back of his hand and she moved into the touch like a magnet finding its north. He hesitated but he'd gone too far to stop. 'Ginny, I'd like to marry you.'

It was a dumb proposal, he thought. He knew it the moment the words were out of his mouth and he saw her flinch.

'Marrying me means taking on Madison as your daughter,' she whispered. 'Fergus, are you sure you can do that?'

'Maybe…'

'You see, there's no maybe about it,' she said, and suddenly she sounded angry. She rose, backing away from his touch as he rose with her. 'This is a crazy conversation. You know it's much too soon. We hardly know each other. We need to go home. Can you help?'

'Of course I can help.' But could he? This is what this is all about, he thought. Ginny had a brother and a child and three dogs. She couldn't handle them on her own. Marriage to Ginny meant marriage to everything.

'There's a child booster seat in the back of my car,' Ginny said, moving on, marriage proposal set aside. She hesitated. 'Richard was uncomfortable in my little car on the way here. Can we put him in your truck?'

'Fine.' But it wasn't fine. He wanted to spend more time here. He wanted to gather Ginny into his arms again and kiss her senseless and make her see… Reason?

'Dogs first,' she said. 'Dr Reynard, I need your help.'

Maybe she'd seen where his thoughts were headed. Regardless, she'd called him Dr Reynard for a reason. He needed to be practical. Richard needed care. They both needed to move into professional mode.

They left Madison till last. The dogs were easy to load into the truck, as was the detritus from their picnic. Richard was harder. He woke up when Fergus touched his shoulder.

'Time to go,' he said softly, and Richard's face clouded.

'It's never time to go,' he muttered, and turned to look at the moon streaming over the lake. Fergus saw tears slipping down his gaunt face.

'Hey, Richard,' Ginny said, and slipped her hand into his. There was a moment's pause. Fergus stepped back and left them together, letting the moment stretch out.

How to say goodbye to life?

But finally Richard gave a tiny, decisive nod and Fergus saw his grip tighten on Ginny's hand.

'Let's go,' he said.

Easier said than done. He had no strength left to stand. They slipped their arms under a shoulder apiece and somehow manoeuvred him into the front passenger seat of Fergus's vehicle. He should be on a stretcher, Fergus thought, but he also knew it had been important that this night hadn't involved stretchers.

It did involve oxygen, though, and it was a fiddle getting everything in the front of the truck.

'Richard, you're going to have to diet before we come back,' Ginny told him, and that got a weary grin. But then he winced. He wouldn't be in physical pain, Fergus knew. He'd been so careful at monitoring medication that he knew there could be little breakthrough. But there was more pain than merely physical.

'Ginny,' he whispered, and Ginny held his hand tight.

'Can you put Madison in my car while I stay with Richard?' she asked, and Fergus hesitated. Richard needed Ginny.

'You drive Richard home in my truck,' he said. 'I'll follow with Madison.'

'If you're sure,' Ginny said. She looked down into her brother's face. 'Maybe we could drive right round the lake.

Miriam will be at home to help you put Madison to bed. And she trusts you, even if she wakes up.'

She did, Fergus thought. She had no choice. She'd been thrust into a family she didn't know and she had to take what was thrust at her.

Including him.

'That's fine,' he said, and something must have shown in his face because Ginny hesitated.

'I don't like—'

'I'll be fine,' he said, making his voice definite and motioning with his eyes for Ginny to say nothing more in Richard's hearing. Richard needed this time so badly. There was so little time left.

'Thanks, mate,' Richard whispered, and Fergus wondered how much he guessed.

Hell.

So they left and all Fergus had to do was lift the sleeping Madison into his arms, carry her over to the car and lower her gently into the child seat...

But as he did so, she stirred. She hardly woke up, but she roused enough to know that she was being carried and she knew enough to make herself more secure.

She sighed, a weary sigh of a child who'd been through too much and had found no joy at the other side.

She lifted her arms, she twined them around his neck and she huddled tight.

As if she was finding her security. Any security.

He cradled her against him as he carried her to the car and she felt...she felt...

Don't think it.

'It's OK, sweetheart,' he whispered into her hair. 'I'm taking you home to bed. Home with Ginny and your daddy.'

'Daddy,' she whispered, and the word cut through him like a knife.

Molly...

Somehow he managed the short drive, but the knowledge

that there was a child right behind him, as there'd been a child right behind him for the last six years except for three empty months made him feel…empty. Blank. Like he didn't know how to go on.

He concentrated on the road ahead. Kangaroos jumped out of nowhere around here. He needed to concentrate.

'I want my mummy,' the little voice whispered from the back seat, and his heart clenched.

'Ginny will be home.'

'I want my mummy.'

No substitutes. He knew how she felt. God, he knew how she felt. That she wasn't Molly…

He pulled into the farmyard and Miriam was on the back veranda, waiting for him.

'Richard and Ginny are coming home the long way in my truck,' he explained. 'They'll be here soon.'

'Let's get the bairn to bed,' Miriam said, accepting things fast for what they were. 'I'll pull the sheets back. If you'll just carry her in…'

'Will you—?' he began, but she'd already turned away.

He opened the car door and unclipped the child harness.

'Bedtime,' he whispered, and once again her arms wound round his neck and she clung.

He carried her up the stairs in silence. The whole night was silent. The dogs were in the back of his truck, being ferried around the lake. Miriam was out of sight, doing what had to be done.

Madison clung and sighed, and his heart twisted until he was sure it must break all over again. As it had broken the night he'd said goodbye to Molly.

How could he think…?

He couldn't. He just…couldn't.

Madison's bed was waiting. Miriam was holding the sheets back.

'I'll change her into her pyjamas if she wakes up and needs to go the bathroom,' she said. 'But it won't hurt her to sleep in what she's in.'

She was in a tiny version of what Ginny was wearing. Soft fleecy pants and windcheater.

He gazed down at her tiny face and he saw a likeness to Ginny. Fleeting but there.

Family.

She snuggled her face into the pillow, and her arms came out, still almost in sleep. This was an involuntary movement, made maybe every night as a sleeping chid was carried to bed.

'Cuddle night,' she whispered, and he had no choice but to put his face down on hers, kiss her gently and give her a soft hug.

She hugged him back. She couldn't be mistaking him for her mother now, he thought, dazed. He had a stubbly chin. He'd smell different. He'd feel different.

'Daddy,' she whispered, and settled back into sleep.

It was half an hour before Ginny arrived.

'We drove right round the far side and watched the moon until Richard slept,' Ginny told him, slipping silently from the truck and going around the back to release the dogs. 'I'm sorry you had to wait.'

'It's OK,' he said, but something about his voice must have changed.

'What is it?'

'Nothing. Let's get Richard to bed.'

The next few minutes were taken up with the mechanics of getting one very ill man into bed, settled, rewired.

'I'm setting up a subcutaneous line,' Fergus told Ginny. He'd watched how much Richard had—or hadn't—consumed during the evening and he knew he'd be getting really dehydrated very soon. Eating and drinking were now too much trouble.

They'd spoken about this to Richard. He wanted no heroic rescues or anything as intrusive as nasal gastric feeding, but dehydration had been explained to him and he'd agreed to fluids when the time came.

'I'm with you on that one,' Ginny said. 'I talked to him about the need for it this afternoon and he said when you said he needed it then it was fine by him. You're his doctor, Fergus.'

He was and he couldn't walk away now. Over the next few days he'd be back here over and over again. But if he had a choice...

'What's changed?' she said. With Richard settled, they'd walked down to his truck. Miriam sat up on the veranda, watching her charges, but she was out of earshot and even if she hadn't been, Fergus knew that anything he said here would never be repeated.

This town knew everything about everyone already. There was no need for eavesdropping. Miriam probably knew already what he was about to say right now.

'Ginny, I can't...'

'You can't be with me,' she whispered. 'I know that. I told you.'

'I thought—'

'Fergus, you're not thinking,' she interrupted, and she laid her hand on his arm and pressed. 'You're hurting. You and I had a wonderful one-night stand. That night set things free for me in a way that I could never have imagined. But it didn't set you free. And my freedom doesn't mean I'm taking things further with you. You're where I've been for years. Running from encumbrances. There's no way I'll load you with mine.'

'But you—'

'Fergus, I'm a package deal,' she said softly, and she lifted his hand and held it against her face. 'I think...I think you're a wonderful man. A man I'd love to love. But there's lots of things to love in this world and you're only one of them.'

'Gee, thanks,' he said blankly, and she managed a shaky laugh.

'Don't mention it.'

'It's only Madison.'

'No,' she said softly. 'It's nothing to do with Madison. You think you'd like to be with me if only you didn't have to look at a child again. But you don't really want to be with me. Not how...not how I want to be with you.'

'I don't understand,' he said miserably, and she smiled and reached up and kissed him lightly on the lips.

'That's because you haven't had an epiphany,' she whispered. 'I hope one day you have it. For your sake. Somehow you've given it to me.'

'An epiphany…'

'I used to try and drive away pain by anger,' she said. 'Or work. Dive into medicine and don't think of anything else, and when the world got too grim I'd go to the gym and kick-box.'

'Kick-box?' He stared and she grinned.

'Didn't know that about me, huh?'

'N-no.'

'Puts me in an altogether new light.'

'Maybe,' he said faintly, and her smile faded.

'Look, it doesn't matter. All I'm saying is that by loving you I realised that it works. I can love again. I can make this life work for me. I can be happy again, even if I've lost.'

'Yeah, but—'

'This isn't about you,' she said. 'What I'm saying is about me. You look at Madison and you cringe inside and there's no way you should put yourself in that position. We go back to being professional colleagues, Fergus. Maybe in a few years you'll have your epiphany and maybe I'll be sitting in my rocking chair with my knitting and my dogs and I'll spend a little part of my pension on another rocking chair so you can sit beside me.'

'Lie beside me,' he growled, and she chuckled.

'I'm betting you'll be a very sexy octogenarian.'

'Ginny—'

'Enough.' She kissed him again, lightly but with purpose. 'We both know this isn't going to happen now for us. Face it, Fergus, and move on. I love you but I don't need you. I wish that could make the loneliness better for you but I don't think anything can. Except maybe time. So give it to yourself, Fergus, love. Walk away.'

CHAPTER ELEVEN

RICHARD died eight days later.

Fergus had been back at the house many times in the interim, but he'd kept his visits relatively formal. With Ginny.

With Richard he'd established something that was as close to a friendship as could be made between people in such disparate circumstances.

'You'll look out for Ginny for me, mate,' Richard had whispered in one of his last few moments of consciousness when Fergus had been by his side. Ginny had been out visiting one of the community's new mums and had taken Madison with her. 'She's playing hardy but when the others died… She breaks up inside,' Richard had told him.

Fergus knew what that felt like. He thought of a grief-stricken Ginny and thought if he only had the courage…

To take Ginny, to take three dogs, to take one little girl…

'I'll keep in touch with her,' Fergus said. 'Though I'm not sure…'

'You don't have to be sure it'll lead anywhere,' Richard whispered. 'And you don't have to be scared either. Take it from me, there's nothing to be afraid of. You know, a few weeks ago I was terrified. But not now. I've been given this place. I've been given the gift of knowing I have a kid and Madison's going to be great. Great for Ginny. Great for…' He paused and his gaze turned inward, as it did increasingly. 'Well, who knows who she'll be great for. But, Fergus…watch out for her for me.'

'I will,' Fergus promised, and when Tony rang him at two in the morning to say it was over, he remembered his promise as he drove through the darkness.

To what?

To a deathbed.

In such circumstances it wasn't even necessary for a doctor to attend. Richard had been in a coma for the last three days. His death had been inevitable. The local undertakers could come and do their job without him, and Fergus could sign the death certificate in the morning.

But not to go now was unthinkable.

He pulled into the yard and Tony was standing on the veranda, waiting for him.

'I knew you'd come,' he said in satisfaction. 'Ginny said not to call you but—'

'But I'd said call,' Fergus said, almost roughly. In truth, he'd wanted to be here himself at the end, but time of death was totally unpredictable and Fergus was employed to take care of the needs of the entire community. Not just one man.

Or one man's sister.

'Was it OK at the end?' he asked. There were deaths and deaths. He'd worked hard to make this one right. He'd rung a Sydney palliative care physician. He'd double-checked himself every way. Please…

'He just slept into it,' Tony reassured him. 'If Ginny hadn't been sitting with him, holding his hand, we wouldn't have known exact time of death. He just slipped away.'

'Ginny…'

'She's not here,' Tony said. 'She said she needed to be by herself for a bit. She left in the car a couple of minutes ago.'

Hell.

He needed to see the whole picture. He needed not to focus just on Ginny.

'Madison?'

'She's sound asleep. We thought we wouldn't wake her.'

'No.'

'You want me to call the undertaker?'

'There's time,' Fergus said. He checked Richard's body but it had been like Tony had said. He'd just slipped away, leaving his body like an outer husk of what had once been there. A peaceful death.

'Can you stay on a bit longer?' he asked Tony, and Tony smiled and shrugged.

'We agreed this was a part of our regular shift work. Madison's on the books as well as Richard. I'm on duty until seven.'

'Ginny will be back by then.'

'You'll go and find her?' Tony asked, and Fergus could see that he was troubled.

'You think I should?'

'I think you should,' the big nurse told him. 'Mate, I think you have to.'

She was in the boatshed. He'd guessed she would be, but even so it was a relief when he pulled into the clearing and saw her car.

The door of the boatshed was open. He pushed it wide and saw her. She was at the other door, sitting on the ramp which slid down into the water. She wasn't moving. For a moment he thought she was in control, simply sitting staring out over the lake.

But then her shoulders heaved with a convulsive sob and he moved like a shot from a gun, kneeling, gathering her into his arms, holding her, pulling her against his chest, taking the brunt of the wrenching sobs as she wept her heart out for the brother she'd loved.

She wept and wept, until it seemed she could weep no more, and then she subsided against him, spent.

He kissed the top of her head and she shuddered, a long, racking shudder that seemed to go right through her.

And then she pulled herself away from him. Her face was almost colourless in the moonlight. Almost deathlike.

'You're never ready,' she whispered, and he nodded.

'No.'

'I thought…'

'That this would be different? You love Richard. How can a loss of a love be anything less than that?'

'Oh, God…'

He couldn't bear it. He couldn't bear it for her.

And here she was opening herself up again for future pain. She'd taken on Madison. She'd taken on three dogs.

She'd take him on if he only could…

He couldn't. He stared down into her face and the grief he saw was a reflection of the pain that had torn him apart for months. To take on more…

She saw it and she withdrew. Just a little. Just enough to show that she'd get past this, she knew it. The control was there, ready to slip down.

She might hurt as much as she'd done before, but maybe she'd learned that she'd survive.

A lesson he hadn't learned yet?

'Thank you for coming,' she whispered. 'I shouldn't have needed…but I did.'

'Of course you did.'

'See. That's the problem,' she managed. 'I'll always need. That's why…'

She shook her head as if ridding herself of a bad dream and tried to struggle to her feet. He was before her, lifting her, supporting her as she made her knees firm under her.

'I'm fine. Thank you for being here for me, Fergus. I'll go back to the house now. I need to get the undertaker before morning. I don't want Madison to be awake when…' She took a deep breath. 'There's things need doing.'

'Let me help you.'

'You've done enough,' she told him. 'You gave Richard the best medical care possible. More, you gave him friendship…'

'But—'

'You have nine weeks left in this place,' she told him. 'I understand you came here to get away from…strings. If you wanted to leave now, I could understand.'

What was she saying? Leave everything, including his medicine? 'I signed a contract.'

'Yes, but I'm available to be medical officer for the district now.'

'Not yet,' he told her, finally finding some ground he was sure of. 'You need time to adjust. Madison needs time...'

'Maybe,' she said. 'But maybe not. This is a new life. Maybe all we need to do is jump right in.'

'But not tonight,' he said roughly, grasping her arms.

She stared down at his hands on her forearms and then very gently she pulled away.

'Yes, tonight,' she whispered. 'That's all there is to do. Jump right back in at the deep end. Tonight.'

Luckily for Fergus, the next two days were extraordinarily busy. The medical scene was hotting up—mostly as the surrounding community realised there was a real doctor who could give real consultations and they didn't have to travel.

To say he was beginning to be overwhelmed was an understatement.

'I can't leave all this to Ginny,' he growled to Miriam the morning of Richard's funeral, and she smiled and shrugged.

'Before you we had no one and we coped. We're blessed that Ginny's agreed to stay here. Do you think we'll stand by and see her worked into the ground?'

'But she won't say no,' he growled. 'I know her. Look out in my waiting room. Who would I say no to?'

'We'll protect her,' Miriam said gently. 'You'll go back to your life and we'll get on with ours. With Ginny.'

And never the twain shall meet. Why did that hurt?

'Meanwhile, you have a queue of six patients, Dr Reynard.'

'Just make sure I'm clear for the funeral at two,' he muttered, and she nodded.

'Of course. As I said, we do look after our own.'

'I'm not your own.'

'While you're going to Richard's funeral, yes, you are.'

* * *

He'd thought the funeral would be tiny. It was anything but.

The church itself was tiny, an ancient grey stone building covered with a mass of briar roses that almost buried it. Miriam and Fergus drove up together, having stopped on the way to check on Ginny.

'We're fine,' she'd told them. She'd been sitting on the back step dressed in a flowery chintzy dress that hadn't looked in the least like a funeral, and she had been holding onto Madison, dressed in much the same way. 'The undertaker's picking us up.'

'Let us take you,' Fergus had urged, but she'd shaken her head.

'Madison and I are family. We'll do this by ourselves.'

She'd looked defiant and brave, and only the pallor of her face had given away the true way she was feeling.

And now...

'She'll have to face the whole community,' Fergus said as they pulled up at the church. 'Alone.'

'She's not alone,' Miriam said. 'The undertaker is Sam Leith and he went to school with Ginny's dad. This is where she belongs. We're her people.' She gazed around the car park. 'There'll be some who are here simply out of curiosity.' She grimaced as she saw Oscar in a wheelchair with a group of half a dozen residents of the nursing home. 'Many of the oldies will be here because they knew Ginny and Richard's grandparents and parents. Many will be sympathetic, though there's always a few who think a funeral's a good excuse for an outing and a free drink or six. And then there's Oscar,' she went on, before Fergus could interrupt and ask. 'He'll be here because he hates the family. Did you know Ginny's mother refused to marry him? Wise woman. Anyway, it's always rankled and he'll be pleased another Viental's dead. But he's an exception. Most of this community will be here because they know Ginny wants to stay here—that she's decided she belongs.'

'But it's so soon.' He'd pulled into the last available parking space behind the church and now he was looking back along the road to where a stream of cars was still arriving. 'And Madison... Should she be coming?'

'Ginny talked to the child psychiatrist,' Miriam said, as if this had been a major source of discussion. 'She said it'd make it much easier for Madison later on if she has some shadowy memory of what's happening. Ginny and Richard brought her together to her mother's funeral. Judith and Richard will be buried side by side. It'll give Madison some sort of link.'

'But today...'

'Is going to be hard for both of them,' Miriam agreed.

'If she'd let me be there...'

'You know, maybe she would,' Miriam said softly. 'But if she let you...would you stay?'

'I don't know what you mean.'

'I think you know perfectly well what I mean,' she retorted. 'If Ginny lets herself lean on you now, she's going to need you for always. That's not what you want now, is it?'

'No,' he said. 'At least...I don't think so.'

By the time they walked into the church the place was packed. People were being directed to the hall next door where a video link had been set up, but as they made to turn away, the usher called them back.

'There's a pew for the medical staff who treated Richard,' he said. 'Second from the front on the left.'

So Fergus sat between Miriam and Tony and Bridget. The organ was playing gentle waiting music. The church was hushed.

Out the front was the coffin, burnished oak and beautiful, loaded with the same wild roses that covered the church.

The last funeral he'd been to, the coffin had been so much smaller...

There was a touch on his hand and he looked down and Miriam's broad palm was covering his.

'Hang in there, kid,' she told him, and he looked at her in wonder. How much could be read on his face?

He'd come to Cradle Lake to hide. How could he hide here?

'She shouldn't be bringing Madison,' he whispered, miserable that he hadn't been able to talk about this with Ginny. But every attempt at contact over the last days had been met with a gentle, 'Thank you, Fergus, we're fine. We need to start as we mean to go on—Madison and me. Let us do this on our own.'

'She's bringing Madison,' Miriam whispered. 'I told you. The child psychiatrist talked her through it. They have a plan.'

A plan. The idea should have made him feel better.

It didn't.

Then a stir at the back of the church made him turn. Sam, the undertaker, was there. And Ginny and Madison and...

Dogs.

Three dogs, all garlanded with flowers. Wearing garlands, woven ropes of flowers of every description.

Ginny and Madison were bedecked with flowers, too, the flowers of their dresses augmented with the gay garlands round their necks. Madison had a circlet of roses in her hair.

Woman and child, dogs and flowers... The church gasped as one.

In they came. Ginny had the whippet and the collie—Twiggy and Snapper—and Madison held the smaller Bounce as if this was a very serious responsibility. The two girls and three dogs made their way in dignified style down the aisle behind the grey-suited undertaker. There was a momentary pause as Snapper decided to cock a leg on a pew—he was clearly only at the beginning of dignified dog behaviour training. There was no consternation, however. Sam was carrying a vast armful of flowers, posies and wreaths of all description. Snapper paused. Ginny paused. Madison sucked her breath in with four-year-old indignation and said, 'Bad dog, Snapper.' But clearly this eventuality had been rehearsed. Ginny simply lifted a pile of flowers from Sam's arms and laid the pile over Snapper's spot. More flowers in a church that was redolent with flowers.

The congregation giggled.

That set the flavour of the entire ceremony.

Richard had had friends. For these last few weeks he'd

wanted to be alone and he'd asked them not to come, but they were here in force now, celebrating his life as Ginny had obviously agreed that they should. There was music—fabulous music. There were people telling wonderful stories of the Richard they'd known and obviously loved. There was a boy, maybe only sixteen, accompanied by his parents, who'd met Richard in hospital some years before and who spoke of the way Richard had made him see that a life with cystic fibrosis could be a great life.

Short didn't necessarily mean empty.

Short just meant stacking more in, living for every moment. Living for now.

And then Ginny and Madison rose, accompanied by their dogs.

'It's time to say goodbye to Richard,' Ginny said softly. 'Your friend. My brother. Madison's daddy.' She smiled gently at the little girl whose hand she was holding. 'Madison, do you want to say what happens now?'

'We bury the shell,' Madison said, holding on for dear life to Bounce's collar with one hand and Ginny with the other, but her clear little voice reached out through the sound system and filled the church. 'My daddy and my mummy were in shells like snails.' She looked up at Ginny for reassurance, but she kept gamely on. 'We've all got shells,' she said. 'Like snails. My mummy said I've got a pretty one with nice hair, and Bounce has got a fuzzy one with stiff hair like a hearth brush. My Mummy said we have to enjoy every minute of being in our shells. She said we should stay in our shells till we get really, really old, and probably that's what'll happen to me and Ginny and Bounce and Snapper and Twiggy. But sometimes we get sick, like my mummy and daddy, and we come out of our shell early. Ginny says that's OK. She thinks my mummy and daddy might have found a new shell together. That's sad 'cos we don't know where that new shell is, but we still have to bury the old shell and that's what we do now.'

What child psychologist had worked their wonder here? Fergus wondered, dazed. What medical textbook did this come from? Judith and Ginny between them? Madison's mother and Madison's new mother. Two redoubtable women.

There was a sniff beside him and the clutch on his hand tightened. 'Oh, Fergus,' Miriam quavered, and he would have given her his handkerchief but he needed it himself.

'That's what we have to do,' Ginny said softly into the hushed—except for sniffing—silence. 'We need to say goodbye to Richard and bury his shell.'

A guitarist—one of Richard's friends—started to play. Six more of Richard's friends separated from the congregation to act as pallbearers and Ginny and Madison and dogs led the way out into the sunshine.

It was over.

Afterwards refreshments were served in the church hall. It was more like a party than a wake, Fergus thought. He couldn't get near Ginny. He stayed for more than an hour, an outsider watching. In the end he was almost desperate for a medical emergency to draw him away, but his beeper stayed silent and he couldn't leave. He just…couldn't.

So he stayed and he watched as Ginny smiled her way through the afternoon, greeting people over and over, listening to anecdotes of Richard's life, being polite, trying desperately not to sway with weariness.

He could see exhaustion seeping in but there was nothing he could do about it. The only time he approached her, her smile had slipped and she'd said with something akin to desperation, 'Go away, Fergus. I don't need you. I can't. Please. Just go away.'

So he'd gone away, but not far. He'd made small talk to other people and he'd tried not to look at her.

Instead, he'd watched Madison.

It had been an extraordinary performance, he thought, recalling the way she'd spoken to everyone in the church. For a four-year-old to speak like that…

She was the only child of a single mother, and he recognised the result. Judith must have talked to this little one as an equal. She must have needed Madison almost as much as Madison had needed her. The result was a child who was older than her years.

But she could still revert.

Tony's children were here, and others. Richard's friends were in the age group who had young children and there were maybe a score of youngsters in the hall. Doing what kids do when grown-ups were boring. Amusing themselves.

The overflow of flowers had been brought in here, set up in vast urns or simply lain in fabulous colourful piles around the walls. Looking at Madison's garland in envy, some of the older children had set up a cottage industry. The older ones had taught the younger ones, and now the funeral flowers were being made into daisy chains. Daisy chains with a difference. Instead of daisies, every single flower imaginable was put into use.

The children made garlands for themselves and then they moved on to parents and aunts and uncles and friends, and finally every single person in the hall was being decorated with Richard's flowers.

It was fantastic, Fergus thought, and the remembrance of his own little girl slipped back. Molly would have loved this. Molly, who'd slipped from her shell too soon...

But she'd had a wonderful life.

As the afternoon settled so, too, did a part of his pain. Madison's words echoed over and over in his heart.

'We have to enjoy every minute of being in our shells.'

These children were doing just that. Making flower garlands from funeral flowers.

He watched Madison, intent on her flowers. Too old for her years, she was intent now on reverting to childhood.

Enjoying every minute of her time...

He could help. He could...

'It's a pity you can't stay on in the valley,' an elderly lady was telling him. 'You know, this place is calling out for two doctors. You and our Ginny'd make a ripper medical team.'

Yes, we would, Fergus thought, but it wasn't just the medical concept he was thinking of. It was as if the fog he'd been moving in for the last few months was lifting, and outside the fog was…

Life?

'We'll have to think about it,' he said absently to his conversation partner. Madison had just completed her garland and he wanted to see what she did with it.

She'd been lying full length on the floor, totally committed to the job at hand. Now she looked up, scanning the hall, looking to see which of the adults were not yet decorated.

Most were. The older children were working faster than the littlies and the production line was becoming efficient.

Ginny was wearing no less than six garlands. Fergus had two. The lady he was talking to had three.

At the far end of the hall the men had set up a bar. He watched as Madison searched the crowd, looking for a bare neck.

Oscar.

He was in a wheelchair, soaking up the free booze. What was the man doing here? Fergus though in irritation.

Madison started to move toward him.

Fergus moved to intercept. He didn't trust…

'Doc, if you're not going to stay, at least tell us where you'll be practising in the city,' the lady beside him said, and she grasped his arm as he tried to move away. 'My daughter lives in Sydney and her doctor's terrible. Last week she had three children down with chickenpox and could she get her doctor to do a house call? I don't think so. And the migraines she gets… You have no idea.'

Her grip on his arm was insistent. Fergus was too late to stop Madison. She's already reached Oscar.

Let the man be gracious, he thought. Let him accept his garland and get on with his drinking.

The garland caught Oscar by surprise. Because he was in a wheelchair, Madison could reach. She simply slipped up behind him and the garland plopped over his head.

He spilled his beer, swore and swivelled.

What happened next Fergus couldn't tell. He was too far away to hear.

But the man grabbed the child by the arm, hauled her up so his face was right in hers and spat words at her that made her blench.

And then he almost threw her aside.

Others were closer than Fergus. Tony reached her first, sweeping her up as one of his own, hugging her, letting her bury her face in his shoulder and carrying her back to Ginny.

That should be me, Fergus thought, struggling through the crowd, and the surge of certainty was so great that he felt almost overwhelmed by it. It was as much as he could do not to haul over there and grab the little girl from Tony's arms.

But she needed Ginny. Already Ginny had gained her trust, and when Tony reached her Ginny held out her arms and Madison crumpled into them and sobbed her heart out.

There was nothing for Fergus to do. Except...

He was right by Oscar now, hardly aware how he'd got there.

'What the hell did you say to her?'

'Nothing,' Oscar muttered, and held up his empty glass. 'Get me another. Bloody kid spilled my drink'

There was a nurse close by—a girl who'd come with the six nursing-home residents. She moved forward, unsure, and Fergus motioned her closer. 'I want Mr Bentley back in the nursing home,' he said through gritted teeth. 'Now.'

'You can't tell me—'

'The only reason you're not being prosecuted for cruelty to animals is that you pleaded disability,' Fergus snapped. 'The inspectors spoke to me and I was forced to confirm it. But if you're well enough to attend funerals, if you're well enough to get drunk on free beer and to abuse young children, then you're well enough to stand trial over neglected horses and dogs and sheep.'

'You wouldn't—'

'Watch me,' Fergus said, through gritted teeth. He glanced up and found Miriam. 'Miriam, could you arrange Mr Bentley's transportation now?'

'I'm on it now, Doctor,' Miriam told him, grabbing Oscar's

wheelchair and propelling it toward the door with savagery. 'The hospital's downhill from here. Permission to stand at the door and push?'

They didn't know what had been said to the child. No one had caught it. Whatever it had been, though, it was as if Madison's fragile shell had been shattered. She was limp and unresponsive in Ginny's arms and her bravado had disappeared completely. This was the Madison of three weeks ago.

'I need to take her home,' Ginny said, and Fergus agreed. 'I'll take you.'

'Sam has the official car at the door,' Ginny said gently. 'Fergus, leave us be. Please. We need to start as we mean to go on.'

With Ginny and Madison gone, the wake was over. Fergus's cellphone rang and it was a woman from Ginny's antenatal class with a threatened early labour.

'I'm only twenty-eight weeks,' she quavered into the phone. 'Oh, Doctor, we want this baby so much.'

Of course she did, Fergus thought grimly as he climbed into his truck and returned to medicine. Why wouldn't you want a baby?

Why wouldn't you want a child?

It was as if the medical needs of the community had been put on hold for the funeral and wake, and now, with it over, the queue was suddenly enormous.

Fergus tried his best to stabilise the young woman and then bailed out, calling in the air ambulance to transport her to Sydney. Maybe his efforts to stop the labour were enough but maybe they weren't and prem babies had a habit of coming in a hurry. In Sydney a twenty-eight-week baby had a chance. Here there were no facilities for premies.

If we had two doctors here, he thought, but he got no further than that as his phone was running hot. A cow had stood on a foot. A urinary tract infection had suddenly become unbearable. Someone was drunk and drifting in and out of unconsciousness and the local policeman wanted him checked before letting him sleep it off in the cells.

Ginny would have to cope with this alone when he left, he thought as he worked on into the evening. Plus she'd need time with Madison. Madison needed a huge commitment if she was to revert to the little girl she should be.

The vision of her in church stayed with him, a tiny girl who'd held the responsibilities of the world on her shoulders.

What had Oscar said to her to make her disintegrate?

He didn't go near Oscar. 'He's fine,' Tony told him. 'Settled back into his bed with a self-satisfied smirk. Why he had it in for that family…'

'It's going to be hard for Ginny to have to keep caring for him here,' Fergus said, and Tony grinned.

'Yeah, well, there's a few of us have been thinking… We reckon Oscar's asthma makes him needful of a nursing home where there's round-the-clock access to a doctor. This place doesn't qualify. We need to declare he's too sick to stay here. A nursing home in Sydney would be much more suitable, wouldn't you say, Doctor?'

'What the hell did he say to Madison?'

'I don't know,' Tony admitted, his face growing grim. Then he shrugged. 'I hope Ginny can defuse it, whatever it was. Meanwhile, mate, there's another call. Seven-year-old Mathew Torney. He fell out of the top bunk and his mother thinks he's dislocated his shoulder.'

'But Ginny…'

'Some of Richard's friends were going back to the house,' Tony said gently. 'Mate, we can't do anything there any more. You know that.'

No. A child with a dislocated shoulder. Medicine.

Hell.

It was midnight before Fergus finished work. He walked out of the hospital and hesitated.

He so wanted to go to Ginny.

She'd be exhausted. She hadn't slept for days.

She wouldn't need him tonight.

'But tomorrow,' he said into the night. 'Tomorrow, please…'

The call came at two in the morning. He'd been staring at the ceiling and it was as if he'd been expecting it. He lifted the receiver and when he heard Ginny's voice at the end of the line, maybe it was as if he'd expected that, too.

'Fergus.'

'Ginny,' he said softly. 'Love.'

'Fergus, help.'

The tension slammed into him as he heard her fear. He heard her terror.

'What is it?'

'I…'

'Say it,' he said strongly, ridding his voice of all emotion, making it curt and businesslike. 'What's happening?'

'It's Madison.'

'What's wrong with Madison?'

'She's disappeared.'

Five minutes later he pulled up at the farmhouse. Ginny was waiting, standing at the gate, staring hopelessly down the road.

Fergus emerged from his truck and Ginny walked straight into his arms.

CHAPTER TWELVE

AFTER the funeral the little girl had been wan and listless, saying nothing, and nothing Ginny could say had broken through.

Richard's friends had been there, back at the house, wanting to sit on his veranda, wanting to feel close to him, and she'd been hamstrung. They'd driven for hours to be there—some having come from interstate. She hadn't been able to send them away. So she'd cuddled Madison until she'd slept. At seven, when Madison had seemed deeply asleep, she'd tucked her into her own bed and she'd checked her every half-hour or so.

At a little after one a.m. the last of Richard's friends had said goodbye.

Ginny had walked into the house to find Madison's bed empty.

'We'll have people searching from one side of the valley to the other within half an hour.' Ben Cross, the police sergeant, had been there within minutes of being called and was now in organisation mode. 'You're sure the people who were here were OK? None of them could have…?'

'I don't know,' Ginny whispered, appalled beyond belief. 'They were Richard's friends. There were about twenty of them. Some of them I know but some I'd never seen before. I was so careful. I was so worried.'

'Hey, Ginny,' Fergus said, and hugged her tighter against

him. 'This is not your fault, love. Let's just focus on finding Madison. Let's think. She wouldn't run away, would she? Where would she go if she ran?'

'I don't know.' There were car lights coming up the hill. Two cars. Three. Four. Ben's calls for help were being answered in spades. 'She seemed almost happy today. We talked and talked. She was so wonderful at the funeral. And then Oscar…'

'We all saw that,' Ben muttered, not bothering to hide his distress. 'What did he say to her?'

'She wouldn't tell me,' Ginny whispered.

'Maybe it's time we found out.' Fergus put Ginny at arm's length, and held her gaze. 'Love, there are people coming to help search. Ben's here. I think the most important thing I can do is to go and talk to Oscar.'

Wrong, his heart was saying. The most important thing he could do was to hold on to Ginny, for ever and ever and ever.

But if he was to rebuild a family for them all then he had to gather the family members together. Madison was part of his family. He knew that in his heart. Maybe he'd always known it.

'I'll be back as soon as I can,' he told Ginny. 'But I need to go.'

Oscar was sleeping the sleep of the pure of heart. His asthma had receded. The last few weeks of regular meals and limited alcohol had improved his health. He was sleeping in a single room with a view over the valley toward the farm he'd neglected for years, and where half his stock had needed to be put down. Yet no conscience kept him awake. He's a patient, Fergus told himself, and somehow he refrained from shaking the man awake and shouting. Instead, he switched on the night-light behind the bed, touched him lightly on the shoulder and sat down in the visitor's chair, waiting for him to wake gently.

He was doing very well, he thought in some abstract part of him that was able to be dispassionate. The doctor part of him congratulated the part of him that wasn't anything to do with his medicine. The non-abstract part.

The part of him that loved Ginny.

And…Madison?

But Oscar was waking up. 'What do you want?' The big man's voice was slurred with sleep and the after-effects of the alcohol he'd drunk the previous afternoon. 'You wake a man up in the middle of the night to do your bloody tests—'

'I'm not here for tests, Mr Bentley,' Fergus said, still in that strange voice that was all professional and not personal in the least. 'I need to know what you said to Madison at the funeral today.'

'Madison?'

'Richard Viental's little girl.'

'The kid,' he said, his face clearing. 'The Viental kid.'

'That's right.' Still that detached tone. Good, he told himself. Very good. No anger. No shouting. 'When she tried to put the flowers round your neck…what did you say to her?'

His face darkened. 'She spilled my drink.'

'She did,' Fergus agreed. 'I'd be guessing that made you pretty angry. A man's got to have a drink.'

'He bloody does,' Oscar said. 'Bloody nurses…'

'It was good of Ginny to put on free beer for the men today,' Fergus said thoughtfully, and he watched Oscar's face change.

'Her. I shouldn't have drunk her beer.'

'Why not?'

'She's a Viental. They should all be dead by now.'

'Why?' Still the conversational tone. Somehow.

'They've got this bloody disease. That woman… I asked her to marry me, you know. This bloody woman's mother. My farm's four times as big as bloody Dave Viental's and she chose him. Made me a laughing stock. I used to see 'em every time I walked up to the ridge, playing happy families, poor as blasted church mice and being…' He sucked in his breath on an angry hiss. 'Anyway, when the first kid died I thought, Great, this is how it ought to be. She chose misery over me. She could suffer the consequences. Then the next kid died and Dave took off.

'You know what I did then? I went over there, cap in hand,

and said, "You know what, Mary, I'm a big man. I can let bygones be bygones. We'll ship the girl off to school in the city and the other boy'll soon be dead. We can start over the way it's supposed to be." And you know what? She stood there, staring at me like I was a lunatic, and then she started laughing. She laughed and laughed and laughed, like it was so hysterical she couldn't stop, and then that bloody girl came out and grabbed her arm and said, "Come on, Mum, you need to rest." And that was that. I went home and I vowed I'd never go to that side of the ridge again until every last one of them was dead. Every last one…'

Somehow Fergus stayed silent. Somehow the medical side of him—the part of him that could suggest a diagnosis of obsessive paranoia, of a solitary man stuck in the groove of hate for over thirty years—could force the other part of him to shut up.

'And now Richard's dead,' he said conversationally, and Oscar nodded.

'Good riddance.'

'But Ginny…and Madison?'

'They'll have it,' he said, and his hatred sounded awful in the stillness of the night. 'They'll both have this cystic thing. Her brothers are all dead, she will be soon, and this last one… Richard…will have passed it on to the kid.'

'I'm sorry to have to disappoint you.' Fergus was amazing himself. His voice was almost gentle. 'Neither Ginny or Madison have cystic fibrosis.'

'Yeah, but they will.'

'No,' he said, and his voice was suddenly harsher than he'd intended. 'You need two cystic fibrosis genes to be ill. Ginny has one cystic fibrosis gene. That means if she marries someone with a matching gene then she might have an ill child but she herself won't get ill. Madison's clear. She's totally free. A normal little girl with a life expectancy of eighty or more.'

'But her mother—'

'Her mother died of cardiomyopathy. It's an infection of the heart. Like the flu. Madison's no more likely to die of it that you are.'

There was a moment's silence. Then Oscar's breath whistled in through his lips in an angry gasp as he accepted Fergus's words for fact.

'Then they'll live.'

'Yes.' With me, Fergus thought, and the thought was a good one. It was reassuring in the awfulness of what he was listening to. Please, he thought. I just need to get him to tell me…

'So what happened at the funeral to make you angry at Madison?' he asked, and Oscar's fingers clenched into fists on the coverlet.

'Made me sick.'

'What made you sick?'

'All that crap about the Vientals. Everywhere…people saying what a shame it was how all the kids had died, and how she's coming back here now and the kid's staying with her and won't it be great? And then that stuff about shells. "She thinks my mummy and daddy might have found a new shell together,"' he said, mimicking Madison's tone and words from the funeral, and Fergus winced. 'That was what I told her. I told her it was crap.'

'What did you tell her?' Fergus demanded, and if he forgot to keep his voice even it wasn't for want of trying. He thought back to that fragment of time—a little girl slipping a garland of flowers over this man's head, the spilled drink, the fury, the grabbing, hauling her up, spitting the words at her. There'd have been time for so little before onlookers intervened. What could he have said in that short interval?

'Just…' Oscar said, and paused.

'Just?' Fergus was holding his breath. He was trying so hard to contain himself that he felt sick. 'Just what, Oscar?'

'"Your mother hasn't found a shell,"' he spat, lying back on the bed and repeating his words with relish. '"Your mother died in the car. She'll be rotting in the ground or, if there is anything afterwards, she'll be stuck on the road outside the football ground, whinging about her lost lover for ever."'

* * *

He didn't hit him.

Somehow Fergus backed out of the ward and closed the door, then leaned against the wall of the hospital corridor, feeling ill.

Such hate. In the middle of tragedy, to hold such hate to yourself when there was room to move on…

He thought suddenly of Molly, his precious little girl, beaming up to him at bedtime, winding her arms around his neck and kissing him goodnight.

There was room to move on. You should move on, because not to…

He had to move on.

He walked out of the hospital, thinking fiercely. Trying not to muddle thoughts of the future with what needed to be done now.

He stood in the car park and let his gaze wander around the moonlit valley.

The football ground lay to the north, about a half of the way round from the hospital, or a quarter of the way round from Ginny's farm. At night the lights would be on for player practice. Let's assume Madison heard those words of Oscar's and took them to heart.

She'll be stuck on the road outside the football ground.

Madison could see the football ground from Ginny's farm. It wasn't very clear during the day but at night it was lit up like a beacon. Madison would have a very clear idea of where it was.

But the lake was six miles round, and the way from Ginny's farm was rough. There was a better road lower on the lake shore but the road from Ginny's was a milk run, designed to take in every farm. There'd be dogs along the road, Fergus thought, hauling his phone out and starting to dial.

There were people searching already but they were searching the bushland around the farm and the lake below. They were also following the main road back this way, thinking that she might have tried to head back to wherever she thought of as home.

His gut twisted at the thought. Madison.

Madison and Ginny.

Ginny answered at the first ring, her voice tight with strain and hope and terror.

'It's OK, love,' he told her. 'I think I know where she's gone. Let me talk to Sergeant Cross.'

'How—?'

'I talked to Oscar,' he told her. 'Let's not get our hopes up too far but I think we're searching in the wrong place.'

And ten minutes later they found her.

Ginny was in the police car. Ben Cross should have been delegating; he should have been organising others, but those others would take time to get back from where they were searching to try again. Much easier to pile into the police car, put the lights on high beam and head along the track to the football ground.

And there she was.

At first Ginny thought she was imagining it—a sliver of light fading into the shadows at the side of the road the moment the headlights lit the road after a curve. But Ben had seen it, too, and he slammed on the brakes and was out of the car before her.

'Madison,' Ginny called, but there was no answer. But Ben had his huge flashlight and he was searching the undergrowth beside the road. There it was again, that flash of white, the cotton of the little girl's nightie. Ben was through the undergrowth, using his body as a bulldozer, reaching…

He had her, lifting her out of the bushes as one would lift a terrified animal. He handed her to Ginny and Madison held herself rigid in her arms.

'Madison,' Ginny managed, trying to hug her close. 'Sweetheart, you're safe.'

'I want my mummy,' Madison whimpered, and the tiny body stayed rigid.

'She's not here.'

'He said…'

There was the sound of another car, coming fast. Headlights, the car slowing as it reached them and stopping.

Fergus, climbing from the car, his face slack with relief.

'You've found her.'

'Just about where you said she would be,' Ben said, looking worriedly at the small girl in Ginny's arms. This was no happy ending.

'I want my mummy,' Madison whispered again, and shoved against Ginny's body.

Ginny's face crumpled in distress and Fergus reached forward.

'Let me take her,' he said, and he lifted her from Ginny's arms and held her close, brooking no opposition. He'd held Molly when she'd been like this, when she'd been cross with him, which hadn't been all that often, when doctors had been running tests and she'd started to be distressed.

Molly.

His face touched this little girl's hair, his mouth brushing the top of her head in a feather kiss. He sat on the ground, even though it was rough and gravelled and not exactly the place to sit, and he motioned Ginny to sit with him.

Ben had kids of his own. He knew enough to stand back, to give them time.

'I'll radio off the search,' he said, and disappeared into the police car.

'Mummy.' Madison was still rigid but Fergus's grasp was firm and solid, using his body to cradle hers, willing warmth into the shivering child.

'Your mummy's not here,' he said to Madison. 'You know that.'

'The man said…' She hiccuped on a sob. 'He said…'

'I know what he said, but he was wrong,' Fergus said in the tone of someone who wasn't to be argued with. 'Ginny told you what happened to your mummy.'

'Ginny's not a mummy.'

Beside him he heard Ginny draw in her breath and he felt her body stiffen. But she didn't move away. She was sitting next to him, so close that her body touched his. It felt good. It felt…right.

And it gave him the courage to say what needed to be said, right now.

'Ginny's not a mummy yet,' he said, soft and firm and sure. 'But she's very, very close to being a mummy. And she's a doctor. She knows what's right and what's wrong, much more than the silly man who didn't want flowers around his neck.'

'He said—'

'We know what he said, but he was wrong. He was feeling tired and crabby and he'd spilled his drink so he said something that he didn't mean, just to make you feel bad. But you know where your mummy is, Madison. You know she's not in the car.'

'She is.'

'No,' Fergus said, and Ginny's hand was suddenly covering one of his, the one that she could see as he hugged the little girl tight. 'You know how I know? I'm a daddy. Daddies know things. Daddies know that, anyway.'

'Whose daddy are you?' she asked, and he winced, knowing he'd opened up yet another avenue Madison might find distressing. But suddenly the words were there and he knew what had to be said.

'I was Molly's daddy,' he said softly. He hesitated but it might as well be said. It was what was in his heart. 'Molly doesn't need me anymore,' he whispered. 'But I think that you do. If you like, if you want me to, I'll be your daddy.'

Maybe it was wrong, he thought. Maybe it was too soon after Richard. But Madison's relationship with Richard had been fleeting. For Ginny to say to her now that she'd be her mother would be cruel and confusing. But to give her a daddy…

It could give her roots, he thought, hugging her tighter, and then he thought, It could give him roots.

'You're the doctor,' Madison whispered in a voice tinged with doubt. 'You're not a daddy.'

'I am a daddy as well as a doctor,' he said evenly. 'And I love your Ginny. I've been thinking… If it's OK with you, I think we might be a family. I've lost my family. Ginny's lost her family and you've lost your mummy. If we came together, I think we could make a really good new family. All of us. You and me and Ginny and Bounce and Twiggy and Snapper. We could all live together in Ginny's lovely house and we could stay together for ever.'

There was a long silence. Ginny's hand had lifted away in shock. It stayed lifted but suddenly it returned. Ginny's hand rested on his, warm and sure and true, and her other hand came up to touch Madison's soft hair.

'That sounds really good, Madison,' she whispered, and she smiled at Fergus in the moonlight as she said it. 'Fergus has come up with a really good idea. What do you think?'

'I'll never find my mummy,' the little girl whispered, and something in her voice told Fergus that this was necessary grief. Madison was letting go.

'You know where your mummy's shell is buried,' Ginny was saying, smoothing down the tousled hair and moving closer so her own body was lending warmth to the child. 'We'll take flowers to the cemetery every time we want, and if you stand on her grave then I'll bet she can hear us when we tell her things.'

'Like telling her I'm going to live with Snapper and Twiggy and Bounce?'

'Exactly.'

There was a long silence while Madison thought this through. The whole world seemed to hold its breath, waiting for a verdict.

Then, out of the silence, a shattering sob. 'My mummy's never coming back.'

'No,' Fergus whispered. 'She isn't.'

And with that it seemed the dam wall broke. Madison, who'd hardly cried these last awful weeks, who'd been self-contained, rigid, older than her years, sobbed and sobbed and sobbed.

They let her cry her heart out, sitting together on the verge of a gravel road in the middle of nowhere, while one sensible policeman held his peace, stayed back, let them do what they willed.

And finally the sobs eased, and when they did, Madison was curled against Fergus's chest as if she belonged there. Which was how it should be, he thought. It was how it must be. From this day forth.

'OK, Madison,' Fergus whispered as the sobs eased to nothing. He rose, lifting her in his arms but still holding her tight against him, and Ginny rose with them. 'Let's take you home.'

'Home,' Madison whispered, clinging close. 'To my own bed that Ginny said was mine. With Ginny. With Snapper and with Twiggy and with Bounce.'

'Let's not forget me,' Fergus said, trying to keep his voice steady. 'I'm part of this family, too.'

Madison opened her eyes at that, very wide, still tear-filled but gazing at him and then at Ginny. She was completely limp now, trusting them to do with her as they willed.

'And me,' she said. Her bottom lip wobbled a little but then she regained her composure. 'Ginny and Twiggy and Snapper and Bounce and…and Daddy. And me. And…my name is Maddy.'

CHAPTER THIRTEEN

FOUR o'clock in the morning. Time for all sensible people to be in bed.

Maddy had fallen asleep in the car on the way home. The searchers had all been thanked and had gone home. The police sergeant had officially watched Maddy be put to bed. He'd surreptitiously wiped away a tear and issued a stern warning to watch over her, and he'd left as well. The dogs had settled after the excitement.

Ginny and Fergus were sitting on the veranda steps, looking out over the lake.

'You realise this means you have to marry me,' Fergus said, and Ginny blinked.

'That's moving pretty fast.'

'Maddy needs fast. I need fast. Do you have any objections?'

'No,' she said, and he turned and kissed her and nothing else was said for a very long time.

When finally there was room for speech again, Ginny snuggled her head down under his chin—there was a warm little spot right in the curve of his throat where she sort of fitted—and tried to think this thing through.

'Um… Fergus, about marriage…'

'Tomorrow,' he said. 'Or maybe today if we can swing it. Is there a time frame?'

'I think it's a month.'

'That's too long. We need a shotgun wedding. Is Gretna

Green too far? Or Vegas? I hear they do great weddings in Vegas. Elvis and everything.'

'No Elvis. I want dogs as my bridal attendants,' she said serenely. 'Vegas involves quarantine.'

'Rats.'

Her chuckle faded. 'Fergus, are you sure?'

'I don't know anything about quarantine.'

'About me, stoopid,' she said, and felt his body chuckle in response. This must be what paradise felt like, she thought. Home.

Home was where the heart was. Home was here.

'I don't think I can have children,' she whispered.

'Why not?'

'I'm a carrier for cystic fibrosis.'

'And I'm not,' he replied. 'After we had Molly I was tested for every genetic problem under the sun. You need two CF genes to make a CF baby and we only have one between us.'

'No,' she said, and tried to focus through the hazy, blissful bubble she was in. 'But any baby of mine has a fifty per cent chance of being a carrier, like me.'

'Then we'll get them tested,' he said. 'We'll teach them what CF involves and how they need to get their own partner tested.'

'It's not fair to keep this thing going.'

There was a moment's pause. 'You mean…you don't want to have children because your child might carry a gene, and he or she might meet someone else with a gene and they might then have children with CF. That's crazy.'

'It's not crazy.'

'It is crazy,' he said, pulling her against him and kissing her hair. 'It's like banning buses because they kill people. Our babies have the potential to be absolutely fantastic people.' He smirked. 'Your looks and my intelligence…'

She punched him.

'Seriously,' he said, and spent a little more time kissing her to show her just how serious he was. 'Ginny, our marriage will be fantastic. You and I will be a team, providing this valley with a medical service they've only dreamed about. Doctors are afraid of being lone practitioners, but this valley could use a multi-doctor service. I'm betting once we set up a viable service, we'll attract more.

'As for us... We'll employ a wonderful, ruddy-faced housekeeper and we'll restore this house to what it ought to be—a family home. We'll buy dog food in bulk. We'll take in orphan lambs. I intend to grow tomatoes because I've always fancied growing tomatoes. We'll give our Maddy the best childhood a child could ever wish for, and if a lovely brother or sister appears to complete the picture then we'll say thank you very much. What do you say to that, Ginny Viental? My gorgeous Dr Viental. My dearest love?'

'I'd say it sounds like a pipe dream,' Ginny said, and she couldn't keep the tears from her voice. 'It sounds like a fairy-tale happy ending.'

'A happy beginning,' he said roughly, and started kissing her again. 'Just watch this space. Dreams come true, Ginny, love. Life holds promise. I'm a surgeon and I should know. I'm starting operating right now. Operation Family.'

'Dreams don't come true,' she whispered, but she didn't sound sure, and she loved it that he laughed and kissed her still more deeply.

'Yes, they do,' he whispered. 'Operation Family starts right now. We need two doctors at the table. Are you ready, Dr Viental?'

'Oh, yes, my love,' she whispered, and he chuckled again.

'I don't think we need theatre gowns for this operation,' he said thickly. 'Do you?'

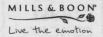
THE DOCTOR'S CHRISTMAS PROPOSAL
by Laura Iding

It's Christmas at Trinity Medical Centre, and nurse Dana Whitney loves the festive season. If only she could get her boss into the Christmas swing! For Mitch, Christmas only brings up painful reminders. Yet there's something about Dana that inspires him. Can he find the courage to love again?

HER MIRACLE BABY by Fiona Lowe

Surviving a plane crash in the forests of Australia sparks the beginning of a real connection between Dr Will Cameron and Nurse Meg Watson. Meg knows she has no future with Will – he wants what she is unable to give him – children. But after sharing a passionate night together, a miracle happens…

THE DOCTOR'S LONGED-FOR BRIDE
by Judy Campbell

It was not until Dr Francesca Lovatt announced her engagement that Jack Herrick realised that he had always loved her. Unable to bear seeing her with another man, he left town. But when he returns as registrar at Denniston Vale Infirmary he finds that Francesca is still single! This time round things will be different.

On sale 3rd November 2006

Available at WHSmith, Tesco, ASDA, Borders, Eason, Sainsbury's and most bookshops

www.millsandboon.co.uk

researching the cure

The facts you need to know:

- Breast cancer is the commonest form of cancer in the United Kingdom. **One woman in nine** will develop the disease during her lifetime.

- Each year around **41,000** women and approximately **300** men are diagnosed with breast cancer and around **13,000** women and **90** men will die from the disease.

- 80% of all breast cancers occur in post-menopausal women and approximately 8,200 pre-menopausal women are diagnosed with the disease each year.

- However, survival rates are improving, with on average 77.5% of women diagnosed between 1996 and 1999 still alive five years later, compared to 72.8% for women diagnosed between 1991 and 1996.

Breast Cancer Campaign is the only charity that specialises in funding independent breast cancer research throughout the UK. It aims to find the cure for breast cancer by funding research which looks at improving diagnosis and treatment of breast cancer, better understanding how it develops and ultimately either curing the disease or preventing it.

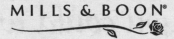

BCC/AD 2006 b

MILLS & BOON®

During the month of October Harlequin Mills & Boon will donate 10p from the sale of every Modern Romance™ series book to help Breast Cancer Campaign continue *researching the cure.*

Statistics cannot describe the impact of the disease on the lives of those who are affected by it and on their families and friends.

Do your part to help, visit
www.breastcancercampaign.org
and make a donation today.

breast
cancer
CAMPAIGN

researching the cure

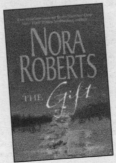

4 FREE

BOOKS AND A SURPRISE GIFT!